Children of the V

by

Elixa Everett

Children of the Vampire King

Cover by: Elixa Everett

The material in this book is intended for ages 18+ it may contain adult subject matter including explicit sexual content, profanity, drug use and violence.

Chapter 1

Julie's hand shook slightly as she closed the cash drawer and handed the burly, fifty-something, silver-haired trucker his change. He was a regular, she was pretty sure his name was Will, but wouldn't have bet money on it.

The trucker looked up her at her with mild concern flashing in his eyes. "You okay, miss?"

Julie nodded. *Get out of here, get out of here fast!* She never spoke the words out loud. Would never dare. *They* would be at the Night and Day truck stop soon. Just because she couldn't see them didn't mean they couldn't see or hear *her*. A chill ran down her spine. It felt as though they had eyes and ears everywhere.

She looked out of the large front window and into the parking lot. The shadows deepened. The sun had almost completely dipped behind the mountain. The only telltale signs of daylight were the streaks of red and orange that filled the near-night sky.

Will nodded. "See you next week, girlie," he waved the two scratch lottery tickets at her as he turned. "Maybe I'll get lucky."

Julie watched him as he strolled out of the store and headed for his big rig. "You have no idea how lucky you already are, mister," she muttered under her breath.

"Have you seen them yet?" A soft female voice came from the direction of the restaurant. It was Sandy, the waitress at the adjoining eatery. There were three people who worked overnights at the Night and Day truck stop: Sandy the waitress, Ricardo the overnight restaurant chef and herself.

They worked every single graveyard shift, seven days a week. They hadn't had a day off in over three months. Not since *they* first appeared. Not that they didn't want time off. Hell, they all would have loved to up and quit, move out of the state of Maryland and never look back. They'd push the nightmare they'd been living far out of their minds.

But they couldn't.

They literally couldn't. The vampires had a hold on all three of them. Regardless of what was going on in their lives, regardless of how physically ill they may be; all three were compelled to be there.

Looking at Sandy, Julie recalled an incident several weeks ago. Sandy had been so sick that she had been admitted into the hospital. However, when eight o'clock came around she was standing in the restaurant in full uniform, gripping the counter for support. It had been heartbreaking for Julie to watch.

The vampires had laughed. They had great fun watching her struggle. Sandy had dropped a full tray of dirty dishes due to being overtaken by a bout of projectile vomiting. This had reduced the four of them to hysterics. Tears had actually formed in their cold, sadistic, red eyes, they had laughed so hard.

"No hun, I haven't," Julie replied with a wry smile.

The only male of the vampire group went by the name of Sebastian. He had taken a liking to Sandy straight away, though

Julie was unsure if *liking* was the best word to describe it. It might be more accurately referred to as an obsessive, sexual infatuation.

Julie could understand the reason for his attraction to Sandy. He and every other male that came into the place had the same reaction to her. Sandy was a petite blond girl of twenty. She had the prettiest deep blue eyes Julie had ever seen. *Guess that goes to show, human or vampire, a man is a man when it comes to some things*, Julie mused.

Sandy sighed and nodded, a touch of a smile lit her face, "Maybe they won't show up tonight?" Sandy's hopeful expression was short-lived.

"Speak and you shall receive," Julie stated. Will's red International big rig passed by her vision to reveal the first of the four vampires clearing the woods and proceeding to stroll across the I-95 heading in the direction of the truck stop. Sandy followed Julie's gaze and also spotted the first of the four vampires. With a gasp she scurried back over to the restaurant. It was her attempt to put off the inevitable. It was useless for her to run and hide, Sebastian would find her regardless of where she scampered off to.

The first vampire to clear the woods went by the name of Tabitha. To all intents and purposes she was the leader of the group. She was a tall woman, with chocolate brown skin and dark eyes. She was wearing her normal attire of ripped low rise blue jeans and a tight black tank top. The wind blew her shoulder length curly brown locks around her face wildly. She was easily the most physically stunning, but also the most cunning of the four.

Next to clear the woods was Sebastian. He was the sole male and looked as handsome as sin, with short blond dishevelled hair and forest green eyes. If Julie could get past her intense hatred of him she might have found him attractive. He walked closely behind Tabitha, looking tall and powerful as he strutted across the highway. His attitude gave the impression that he owned the world. In his mind, perhaps he did.

The third to come into view was Chyna, not her real name, but the name Tabitha had decided to call her. Tabitha either didn't care for, or couldn't pronounce Chyna's real name. From Julie's limited knowledge, Chyna had joined the group a few years back. She had been a university student at some prestigious university on the east coast. She had been sent to the United States by her parents in China who had wanted the best for their little girl. Apparently, she had quite a promising future ahead of her. *Had,* being the operative word.

From what Julie knew of her story, Chyna and a group of her college friends had been camping at a little site in the northern part of Maine, when Tabitha and Sebastian had come across their group. The vampires killed her six companions, bleeding them down to their last drop, but spared her.

Tabitha evidently thought Chyna would make a stunning immortal, an opinion with which Julie tended to agree. With her long raven black hair cascading down her back, dark, mysterious black eyes, and slender figure, Chyna was stunning to say the least. She followed the other two with elegance and grace, the skirt of her yellow sundress blew fiercely around her thighs as she walked. She almost always wore sundresses.

Finally, there was Veronica, the newest member of Tabitha's entourage. If Julie could find sympathy in her heart for any of the vampires then it would be for her. Julie had been there the night they had turned Veronica. She had watched the transformation happen, right there in the middle of the truck stop parking lot, just a few weeks ago. Veronica was the poster girl for the phrase *wrong place, wrong time* as far as Julie was concerned.

She remembered that day vividly...

A few weeks ago...

Julie watched as a petite young woman drove up to the Night and Day truck stop in a beat up little blue Sunbird. The vehicle must have been fifteen years old if it was a day. Looking the girl over as she exited the car, the first thing Julie noticed was how tiny she was: barely five feet in height. Her hair was black with thick red streaks throughout, cut into a short bob. She had a number of piercings in her face, a stud in her nose, rings in both lip and eyebrow, and of course a row of gemstone earrings up the length of each ear. She was cute, a little funky looking, but cute nonetheless; and young - perhaps twenty years of age.

The girl headed straight for the coolers grabbing a couple of bottles of soda then onto the junk food. With her selections in hand, she made her way to Julie at the cash register. She plunked her food down in front of her. Two bottles of Coca-Cola, a bag of potato chips and a Snickers bar.

The diet of champions, Julie thought, giving the girl a weak grin.

Julie looked out of the window and, upon seeing the darkening sky, felt a sense of terror. She needed to get this girl out of the store *fast*!

The girl eyed Julie's nametag as she passed over her purchases. "Julie. My best friend back in Arkansas is named Julie," she extended her hand, "I'm Veronica."

Julie hesitantly took her hand, but kept her eyes on the horizon, "Good to meet you. So where are you headed?"

The girl whom Julie now knew to be Veronica smiled, "New York City, I'm going to be an actress."

Only if I can get you out of here in time, Julie mused as she rang up the purchases and recited the total.

Veronica dug through her backpack, which appeared to be doubling as a purse and handed her a number of crumpled bills. "Oh wait, I'm short a quarter." She put her hands to her hips and stood looking over her purchases in thought. Her face lit up and she wagged a finger in Julie's direction exclaiming, "You know what! I think I have one in my car, I'll be right back in a flash." She turned to head back out the door.

"No!" Julie lunged across the counter and clutched at Veronica's arm.

Veronica looked at Julie's fingers, white knuckles digging into her arm, shifted her gaze to meet Julie's anxious eyes then back down again to her arm.

Julie's face went white. "Oh. Umm. What I meant to say was I have lots of change here in the take a penny tray. So don't worry about it. My treat. Just remember me when you become a star."

Veronica gave her an uneasy smile and nodded. "Thanks."

It was at that very instant Julie came to appreciate just how much of a difference two minutes can make in a person's life.

As Veronica gathered her goodies and left the store, heading for her Sunbird, Tabitha appeared from the woods across the interstate. Veronica noticed the first of the vamps and stood as if mystified by her. *Her* quickly became *them* as the others also emerged. She continued to stand, as if rooted to that spot, staring as the other two appeared behind Tabitha.

Julie supposed it wasn't every day you witnessed a group of people who could easily grace the cover of 'Vogue' magazine come strutting out of the woods. Moving on instinct and not sure why she was risking her own neck, literally speaking, to save the girl, but just knowing she had to, Julie ran from the store to the girl's side.

"Get in your car and go!" Julie screamed at the girl, brushing past her, opening the door of the car, and attempted to push her inside.

The girl continued to stand as if rooted to the spot. She simply stood with an expression on her face that a person could easily identify as the "doe in the headlights" look.

Frustrated, Julie gave Veronica's shoulders a shake, which seemed to break the trance she had been in. She blinked, looked at Julie and allowed herself to be hustled into the car, sliding in behind the steering wheel.

"Go, go, *go*!" Julie urged, closing the car door for her, while Veronica fumbled for the keys. Slipping the key in the ignition, Veronica attempted to start the vehicle, but all she got was a clicking sound.

Click, click.

Julie's heart sank.

Again*: click, click.*

"Ohhh Julie," a voice came from behind her, it was soft, sensual and female. She could feel the cool breath on her neck. It sent shivers up her spine. "I must say, I'm really disappointed in you. We'd like to meet your friend there." Julie pivoted around to find Tabitha standing behind her, less than a foot away.

Tabitha motioned with a nod of her head for the others to remove Veronica, from the vehicle. Stepping up to the driver's side of the car, Sebastian took hold of the girl's elbow and pulled her roughly from the vehicle. She attempted to squirm out of his grasp, but it was a useless effort. Brute strength and an extra eighty pounds easily won out.

"Let me go you...you swine," she spat at him with a mixture of terror and anger in her voice.

Julie took a step toward the battling duo only to have Chyna intercept her. With a broad smile on her face, and a devilish gleam in her black eyes, she slowly wagged her finger back and forth under Julie's nose.

Julie looked over at the half dozen or so semi-trucks parked over at the side of the building. She could yell to them, but it would do no good. The only thing it would accomplish would be to get another innocent person killed in the process of attempting to save the girl. She and the girl with the funky hair were at the mercy of the trio.

Without a word, head bowed, Julie took a few steps back. She thought about her two co-workers inside the truck stop. If she caused too much of a hassle for the vamps there would be consequences. Not just for her, but for them as well.

"Fine," she said, her voice barely more than a whisper, however she couldn't keep the sharp edge from creeping into it. Chyna's dark, oval eyes narrowed at Julie; she hadn't missed the edge in Julie's voice either.

The girl screamed. She clawed at Sebastian, her legs kicking violently, hoping to make contact.

They laughed. The fuckers laughed at everything.

"Feisty little one isn't she?" Chyna commented lightly, with obvious glee.

Tabitha stepped up to the left of Julie, wrapping an arm around her shoulders and leaned over to whisper in her ear, "Watch this. We're going to show you how you become one of us."

Julie turned her head to look into Tabitha's dark eyes.

"Trade secrets," Tabitha whispered, giving her a wink.

Lucky me, Julie thought.

Sebastian was finally able to position himself behind Veronica, wrapping her in a huge bear hug, holding her arms solidly against her sides. He had a self satisfied smile on his face.

Big man to be able to subdue a human half your size, you dick, Julie thought, not daring to say the words out loud.

Sebastian's victory was short lived as Veronica ducked her head down and bit into his left forearm.

Startled, Sebastian released her, letting out a yelp of surprise.

A hint of a smile formed on the girl's lips and victory flashed in her eyes. Not wasting a moment, she sprinted for the semi-trucks parked to the left of them.

"Fucking bitch," he roared, as he chased after her. The chase lasted all of thirty seconds before he had tackled her from behind, sending them both sprawling to the ground.

The ordeal had sent the two female vampires into hysterical laughter.

"Having some issues holding onto the little human, Sebastian?" Tabitha taunted. Her taunt was greeted with a snarl from him.

Veronica was screaming now for all she was worth. Her high pitched shrills pierced Julie's ears and at the same time wrenched at her heart. She attempted a half step toward the two only to feel Tabitha's hand grip the back of her neck. Tabitha's fingernails pinched the soft flesh of her neck, coming dangerously close to piercing it.

Julie noticed that the traffic was surprisingly light that evening. She half-hoped a truck would pull in and put a halt to this madness. The other half was relieved no one did, as this girl was surely going to die tonight so anyone who dared attempt to rescue her would be destined for the same fate.

Cars and trucks continued to drive down the I-95, although none took any notice of the group or even bothered to slow down. Chances were, even those who might have noticed had decided it best to keep their noses out of it. Julie was beginning to learn that you tended to live longer if you minded your own business. She seemed to be getting a crash course in *that* philosophy at that very moment.

Julie looked nervously over at the trucks to their left again. All the lights were out in the cabins. No one was awake, in spite of the screaming from the girl or the laughter from the vamps. No one to witness what was happening, except for the five of them and the two faces of her co-workers peering out through the window of the restaurant.

"Be a good girl, Julie." Chyna stepped back and positioned herself to the right of Julie. She reached out and trailed a finger down the length of Julie's arm.

Julie jerked her arm away. The cool chill from the vamp's touch shot through her body as if it were a bolt of lightning. This resulted in a snigger from Chyna, before she turned her attention back to Sebastian and the still struggling Veronica.

Sebastian threw Veronica to the asphalt of the parking lot and stood behind her.

Julie hazarded a look at Tabitha out of the corner of her eye. She was smiling, her eyes had turned blood red and she was focused on Sebastian and the girl, her lips slightly parted displaying her fangs.

From her experiences with the vampires thus far, she understood their eyes remained the colour they were as a human until their emotions were heightened. They then turned a menacing, blood red colour.

Sebastian had hauled the girl back up to her feet, bringing her, twisting and screaming, back to the group. She attempted to bite at the hand that had a death grip on her arm.

"Do that again and I'll rip your fuckin' head off," Sebastian raised his hand to demonstrate his point. As if to challenge her to make him prove it.

She quieted down, and quit struggling though the stare she gave him said it all. Her face was contorted into a look of absolute rage and frustration.

"I think perhaps Sebastian has some unresolved anger issues," Chyna commented to Tabitha as the smirk she wore widened.

"Fuck you," Sebastian retorted, causing both female vamps to break out in another round of laughter. He had finally gotten Veronica under control and was currently standing behind her, one arm securely around her waist with the other across her throat.

At that moment, looking back and forth between Tabitha and Chyna, Julie was reminded of the cackling witches in 'Macbeth', with the obvious exception that neither one looked anything like the old crones from the play.

Julie's heart went out to the girl once more, as she looked at Julie with pleading eyes. They were begging her to do something, *anything*. Julie turned her head away; it was too painful to watch.

"Enough," Tabitha commanded. All went quiet. The sobbing ceased, the laughter, even the world around them seemed to go completely still. She walked up to the girl. Reaching out, she touched the girl's cheek with the back of her hand.

"So soft and warm," Tabitha muttered to nobody in particular.

Tabitha took several steps back from the girl, examining her, taking in each and every inch of the girl's five feet and her one hundred odd pounds. She nodded. "I think she will make a fine addition to our family."

Veronica's large green eyes widened. She began to struggle against Sebastian once more; struggling with every fibre of her being; struggling for her life!

Stepping back, Tabitha reclaimed her spot next to Julie. "Do it," she commanded with a nod and wave at Sebastian.

Without another word, Sebastian took hold of Veronica's head, jerking it to the side, and exposing the tender, lightly tanned flesh. His fangs dropped into place as he lowered his head to her neck, sinking them in and drinking deeply.

Veronica screamed one last time, struggling more violently than ever.

Less then a minute later it was over. Her body sagged against him. The green eyes which had up until very recently shone with life and vigour were now dim and empty.

"You're killing her!" Julie screamed as she attempted to run to the girl's rescue. She hadn't gotten two steps from her spot before a hand shot out and grasped her upper arm, pulling her back. She winced as she felt fingernails puncture her skin and felt the warmth of her blood slowly making its way down her forearm.

"I thought I told you to stay put," Tabitha chided.

Sebastian let the girl fall to the ground at his feet. As Julie watched, she was reminded of a marionette: the girl's legs seemed to simply give out on her, knees buckling inwards, as she collapsed into a heap on the pavement. He then proceeded to bend over her, bite into his own wrist then place it over the dying girl's mouth. The deep red liquid seeped from his wound and into her partially open, pink painted lips. A trickle missed her mouth and left a fine trail of blood running from the corner of her mouth, down the side of her cheek and into her hairline.

A black semi-truck, with the name of Freightliner emblazoned on its grill swung off the highway and made its way to the truck parking area. As much as Julie wanted to believe that the truck meant help was on the way, she knew differently. It simply meant there would be another unsuspecting trucker for them to feed on tonight.

Please don't come over here, Julie silently prayed to the driver. If he minded his own business, they'd simply feed from him, make him 'forget' it ever happened and he'd leave in the morning, with his life. Best case scenario. If he interfered with what was going on in front of him, then she feared that particular trucker wouldn't be making it home to his family after his run.

As Julie watched the truck slide into an empty slot between two other trucks she could hear a gurgling sound coming from the girl. Whipping her head around, she gasped as she took a step backwards. Veronica was bucking and convulsing on the ground before her.

The three vampires stood watching. Watching and laughing. Chyna's laughter rang out above the rest, cold and wicked.

"Is she going to be alright?" Julie knew the answer already, but couldn't help the words from tumbling out of her mouth.

The girl would never be alright again.

"She's going to be better than alright. Better than human," Tabitha whispered in her ear.

Chyna's laughter quietened as she slid an arm around Julie's waist.

Julie froze on the spot at the feel of her cold touch, she wouldn't have been able to move a muscle if she'd tried. She felt the vampire lean in, felt Chyna's breath on her neck.

"One day, if you're a good girl we just might make *you* better than human." Chyna, promised.

Julie tried not to cringe as she felt Chyna's lips graze her neck as she spoke.

"Hey! What's going on here?" A loud, deep voice bellowed from the direction of the truck parking lot. Julie's head, along with those of the three vampires, shot around towards the direction of the voice. The vampires lost interest in the man straight away, but Julie kept her eyes on him.

A very large man, of perhaps three hundred pounds came marching up toward the group. He had what appeared to be a crowbar in his left hand. He reminded Julie of a trucker version of Santa Claus. It was the long white beard that did it. Trucker Santa. She had to hand it to him, for a large man, he was moving towards the group at a frantic pace.

"Sir, its fine. We have this under control," Julie shouted out to him.

The man continued to close in on them, ignoring her reassurance that the situation was contained.

The three vampires turned their attention from the convulsing girl back to the man storming towards them. Their laugher ceased, but amused grins continued to adorn their faces.

"My God!" The man, aka Trucker Santa, gasped as he reached the group and knelt down beside the girl. "Have any of you fools called an ambulance?"

Santa seemed pissed.

"She'll be fine," Tabitha assured him, taking a few steps in his direction.

Julie noticed Chyna and Tabitha share a knowing look, as if anticipating something.

He put a hand up to stop her. "Stay where you are. She needs some space." He leaned closer to the girl. His hand reached out and brushed a strand of red and black hair from her face, just as her eyes blinked open!

Veronica's eyes opened to reveal that they had turned from the bright green to a deep red. Her body stopped convulsing as she sat up.

The trucker leaned back on his heels, giving her space.

"My God," he gasped once more, this time it was barely more than a whisper. With a shake of his head he requested, "Someone go get her some water, she needs some water."

Chyna moved with lightening speed to stand directly behind the trucker, aka Santa. "Sorry. That's not exactly what she needs. But you'll do nicely." With a quick, swift motion she withdrew a knife from the pocket of the brown bomber jacket she was wearing and swiftly made a deep slit across the front of his neck.

The trucker made a gurgling sound as the blood began gushing from the slash in his throat, down his chest and splattered onto his stomach. He clutched for his throat as he began to sway.

"Weebles wobble but they don't fall down," Chyna quipped causing the group to burst out in a new round of sadistic laughter.

But he did fall down. He fell to his right side, his skull smashing hard against the asphalt. The new vampire hissed, her fangs flashed, as she leapt onto the dying trucker. Savagely she tore into his bleeding throat, lapping up the blood greedily.

He was close to death, no longer able to speak, or defend himself from the rapacious assault. The only sound that could be heard at that moment was that of the newborn vampire greedily feasting on the trucker.

Julie turned her head, unable to watch any longer. But what is seen cannot easily be unseen. She suspected she would endure nightmares for years to come. She didn't want to have to consider the poor man dying at the Night and Day truck stop. *Wrong place, wrong time,* Julie thought for a second time that night. Julie found herself hoping he didn't have a wife and children who would miss him.

Looking at the faces of the vampires she saw no remorse or sympathy. All she saw was pure, unadulterated evil, as they watched with glee, the 'weeble wobble' being devoured. She wasn't sure how to stop them, or even if she could. Part of her hoped eventually they would tire of this place and leave the people here alone once and for all.

Looking over her shoulder and into the restaurant window, she could just faintly make out Richardo and Sandy watching from the shadows. She couldn't make out their faces, but was certain they had the same look of shock and horror that certainly must have been evident on hers.

Looking back at the new vampire and the dead trucker, she found herself silently beginning to pray. Praying for the poor girl, who had showed up at the wrong place at the wrong time; praying for the dead trucker, who was only trying to help; and praying for herself, Ricardo, and Sandy. They all needed a miracle, but she wasn't sure if God was listening or even cared.

God has left the building, an alien voice cackled and taunted from a strange, dark place in the back of her mind.

Chapter 2

Present day

The vampire foursome entered the Night and Day truck stop parking lot, heading directly for the convenience store. It was their normal routine. They would enter the store and hang out there during the night, as if they were nothing more than ordinary humans keeping their good pal Julie company.

Each of them would pick one lucky trucker for the night who they would feast upon. They never killed the truckers, they simply fed, then worked their vampire compelling mumbo jumbo on them. The truckers would leave the next day. Work as usual, but feeling like royal shit when they left.

Julie knew they hadn't spared the lives of the humans out of the kindness of their hearts. She knew it had more to do with the fact that they enjoyed hunting and feeding here. So she suspected they didn't want to draw suspicion on the place. The fact of the matter was that the vampires were insane, no doubting that, but one thing they were *not* was stupid. It was all speculation on Julie's part, but she was confident in her assessment of the situation.

Chyna was the first to enter the store. She strode over to the counter, and hoisted herself up onto it, seating herself next to the beef jerky display. Glancing over to her right she turned her attention to a Jolly Pops display, slid a green one of out the dispenser, removed the wrapper and stuck it into her mouth, tossing the wrapper on the floor.

She noticed Julie watching her. "Want one?" she offered sweetly pulling another from the dispenser and offering it to Julie. While her smile claimed friendship, the gleam in her dark eyes was unmistakable. It was the look a cat gets when it's playing with a mouse. The cat looks happy and serene as it tortures the rodent, but if you look into the cat's eyes you see the gleam of sadistic delight. You see the sheer enjoyment the cat has knowing it holds the life of that mouse in its paws.

As Julie exchanged glances with Chyna, she saw that gleam. The gleam that said, *You're only alive because I am letting you live. Because you're fun to toy with, for the time being. So don't stop being fun, for your sake.*

Julie didn't intend to.

Julie shook her head. "No thanks." With a sigh, she leaned forward, resting her elbows on the counter, pretending to look more relaxed and unconcerned by Chyna's presence than she actually was.

Chyna shrugged and placed the Jolly Pop back in the dispenser, "Suit yourself."

Sebastian entered next bellowing for Sandy as he entered.

There was no response.

Sandy, get your ass out here, Julie thought. Nothing seemed to piss Sebastian off more then when Sandy hid from him. It only made his treatment of her worse when he did find her. He seemed to take it as a personal offence, which of course it was.

For the most part, the vampires tended to leave Ricardo alone, and focused mainly on harassing her and Sandy for their nightly fix of "shits and giggles."

"Sannnnnddyyy," he called out once again as Tabitha and Veronica entered the store. Sebastian was about to head into the adjoining restaurant when Sandy came scurrying from it.

Julie hadn't realized she was holding her breath until that moment. She exhaled loudly.

"There's my girl," he welcomed her. When she drew near, he took her hand and pulled her into a tight embrace. One of his hands slid down to her ass, pulling her body tight against his, while the other grasped a fist full of her hair, bringing it up to his nose. He leaned close to her, and breathed in the scent of her shampoo. "Mmm...So very nice."

Julie watched Sandy tense up in his arms, her body trembling from the fright. Julie wished she could take the girl’s place, so she wouldn't have to endure Sebastian's unwelcomed touches, but she couldn't. He wanted Sandy. Only Sandy.

"Slow night tonight," Tabitha remarked as she searched the store, restaurant and adjoining truckers’ lounge which were all empty. Julie had noticed a number of trucks outside with their lights out earlier, but no one had come in for close to half an hour.

"It is," Julie confirmed, trying to look sympathetic. It was a failed attempt.

Sebastian, holding the quivering Sandy in front of him walked towards them. "We could always sample the local cuisine." He bent his head down to the side of Sandy's neck and trailed his tongue up it, from the collarbone to her earlobe. "It's been a long time since I've tasted my sweet Sandy here."

Sandy yelped as she squirmed in his arms, causing him to grin and Chyna to smirk. His fangs dropped into place, and just as he was about to plunge them into the tender flesh of Sandy's neck, Tabitha stopped him.

"Let her be," she ordered.

"Just playing around Tabitha," Sebastian snarled. Giving Tabitha a vicious glare Sebastian retraced his fangs and released Sandy. She scurried away from him to stand behind the counter, next to Julie.

Glancing over at Veronica, Julie almost felt bad for her. Almost. She looked like such a fish out of water. If the vampire foursome could be considered a family, then she was without a doubt, the black sheep of it. She had never seemed, at least as of yet, to have developed the same zest for killing or delight in torturing humans as the others had.

Looking out of the store window, Julie noticed a large emerald green Freightliner semi-truck pull into the truck stop and head for the truck parking. The vampires turned their attention to the truck as well. They watched as it parked, and let out a burst of air, which made a loud whooshing sound as it shut down.

Moments later a small, beat-up little white car pulled into the parking lot.

The door of the car opened and a thin, dark haired woman of average height stepped out. She wore a black skirt which barely covered her rear, stiletto heels and a black corset. She strutted, shoulders back, ample boobs thrust out, towards the newly arrived semi.

"Ohhhhh, lot lizard," Chyna commented as she clapped her hands together in delight.

The vampires particularly loved the lot lizards. Julie supposed for several reasons. Lot lizards were normally never missed so the vampires could simply kill them and dispose of their bodies. In instances like this one, the vamps would simply take the car and dispose of it as well. The how and where of the car and corpse disposal was never revealed, at least not to the humans working at the Night and Day truck stop. It was just a simple fact.

The truth was that she had no idea where they even lived. They changed their clothing and were always bathed so Julie assumed they had a residence somewhere nearby. They always arrived the same way each night, on foot, through the woods and across the I-95.

The hooker rapped on the door of the truck, and waited. Moments later the driver's side door swung open. She climbed up onto the side of the truck and disappeared inside, closing the door behind her.

"We'll wait until she's finished her business with the driver," Tabitha announced.

"Anyone interested in wagering on how long it takes?" Sebastian asked with a grin, his green eyes shining. "I'll give him fifteen minutes."

Chyna removed the Jolly Pop from her mouth and laughed. "Being pretty generous there cowboy; ten minutes tops." She glanced over at the silent Veronica, "What about you? Care to wager?"

Veronica shook her head, her green eyes looking distracted.

"You're such a buzz kill Veronica," she jerked a thumb at Julie's direction, "almost as bad as the human over there."

"Fuck you, Chyna," came Veronica's venomous response.

Chyna focused her attention on Veronica, her dark eyes challenging Veronica's green ones.

A tense silence permeated the store. The only sound Julie could hear was that of the beverage machines and the beating of her own heart. Tabitha took a step forward in the direction of Chyna and Veronica, with the apparent intention of placing herself in between the two vampires.

It wasn't necessary.

Chyna broke out into fits of laughter. Tabitha and Sebastian joined in laughing with her. The Jolly Pop went flying from her mouth and landed on Veronica's scuffed black work boot. At the sight of the Jolly Pop sticking straight up on Veronica's boot, Chyna laughed harder, holding onto her abdomen.

****

As they waited to see who was going to win the bet Veronica glared at Chyna. She hated them all, including Chyna. She was simply an asshole of the worst kind, and certifiably insane to boot. She was reckless. Veronica would bet money that if it wasn't for Tabitha having such a clear head and firm hand on the others, Chyna would think nothing of rampaging through town after town, leaving nothing but corpses in her wake.

Despite Chyna's numerous shortcomings, Sebastian was easily the most despicable, in her eyes. He had raped Sandy on numerous occasions, in fact just recently, though none of the others was aware of it. He had compelled Sandy to forget each of the incidents.

Perhaps she *had* forgotten on one level. But Veronica could tell, by the way she hid from him; by the way she quivered with fear whenever he came near, that on a deeper, darker level, Sandy remembered. Veronica vowed she'd find a way to make him suffer for what he'd done to her, and the hundreds of others like her down the years.

She had not let on to the others, but since she had been turned she had gained the ability to read minds. Minds of humans and vampires alike. The others had asked her, on numerous occasions, if she had developed any ‘powers’, but she always told them no. They responded by telling her that she would, given time.

Tabitha, the leader and oldest of the group was a unique case in Veronica's eyes. She certainly had the bloodlust, and the vicious nature, but she had an abnormal amount of control over her primal urges. In addition, she was smart. Very smart. She kept the others under control, forcing them to restrain their urges to a certain extent. It was her idea to feed at a truck stop, and it was an exceptional idea.

Truckers were constantly on the move and rarely home so those telltale marks on their necks would be healed by the time they arrived home to their loved ones. Also, there was a constant rotating supply of men, and occasionally, women to feed from so they never had a need to migrate to other areas for fear of being discovered. They fed, made the person forget the whole incident and then sent them on their way.

Veronica learned the need to feed well over the weeks. The primal, gut wrenching need for blood could not be ignored, so she actively indulged each night the same as the others. At least until she found a way to get out from under their thumbs.

They made it clear the first night of her new life that she was going to be with them a very long time; if she attempted to leave their little family there would be repercussions. And as she looked over at Chyna, then across the room at Sebastian, she knew that to be the truth.

A short while later they discovered that Sebastian had won the bet. Fifteen minutes later the whore opened the door to the cab and climbed out. Once back on the ground she adjusted her clothing as she headed back to her car. The truck driver, a tall dark haired lanky man exited the cab directly after her. He didn't bother to head toward the store; instead he stood by the door of his truck and took a piss.

Once done, the trucker gave his now limp 'instrument' one last shake before tucking it away.

"Good till the last drop," Chyna commented with a hoot of laughter. The others followed suit, chuckling and cackling along with her.

The whore was now getting back out of her vehicle and heading back towards the trucks, presumably to solicit more business.

"Let's go," Tabitha commanded as she made her way to the store exit. The others quickly followed behind, leaving Julie and Sandy alone. As much as Julie hated thinking it, she was always relieved when they shifted their focus from her and Sandy and redirected it onto the truckers.

The lot lizard stopped in mid-stride upon hearing the foursome walking toward her. Veronica almost felt bad for her. The woman was only trying to make a buck, the best way she knew how.

Chyna was the first to reach her, blocking her path to the trucks. "Hiya," she stood in front of the woman, twirling her long black locks around her left index finger. She had taken another Jolly Pop from the display before she had exited the convenience store. She pulled the wrapper off, tossed it to the ground, and popped the blueberry Jolly Pop into her mouth.

As Veronica approached she could make out the woman's features more clearly now. She was extremely thin, even thinner than Veronica had originally realized. She could see the woman's bones clearly in her arms and shoulders. Her eyes were dark, matching the dark brown colour of her hair.

The woman turned to make a hasty exit for her car, but Sebastian ensured she wouldn't make it back. She sighed in resignation. "What do you want?" she asked, her voice rough, hoarse from too many years of cigarettes and God only knew what else.

"We're hungry," Chyna answered, pulling the Jolly Pop from her mouth to answer, then popping it back in.

"I have no money," she gave a weak laugh, "Just trying to make a living."

"Oh, we don't want money," Sebastian stepped up behind her, grasping her frail shoulders in his hands. He started to lower his head to her neck, but was stopped by the sound of Tabitha's voice.

"Wait!" Tabitha came closer to the woman. She sniffed the air as one might see a hound doing when it smelled its supper. "There is something wrong with her." Tabitha stepped closer, then bent down and pulled a dagger from her boot.

Veronica saw a glint of silver just seconds before the smell of fresh blood assaulted her nostrils. Looking at the woman she noticed Tabitha has made a cut across her upper chest. The blood seeped from the slit, into her cleavage.

"There is something wrong with her blood." Tabitha announced as she drew closer still, her mouth inches from the heaving breasts of the whore. "She's diseased."

"What's wrong with her?" Chyna stepped closer, sniffing the air around the woman. Her face distorted in a look of frustration. It was evident she couldn't tell the difference.

Veronica cocked her head to the side, as if hearing something, listening for something. The others were too transfixed with the whore to pay much attention to her. *HIV-Positive.* She caught the woman thinking. It was then that she remembered seeing a news story about this woman a few weeks ago, before she had been turned. She was what the news channels were calling the New England Mistress.

"She's HIV-positive," Veronica stated, crossing her arms over her chest.

Chyna and Sebastian gasped, stepping away from the dark haired woman.

"Vampire's can't catch HIV you fools," Tabitha chastised, shaking her head at them in a look of disgust, laced with pity.

Tabitha's head shot around to stare, dark eyes narrowed, at the newest member of their group. "How did you know that?"

Veronica hesitated, just catching herself from disclosing that she had read the woman's thoughts. "I saw a news story about her several weeks ago; they're calling her the New England Mistress. She's infected dozens of men over the past few months."

Sebastian smiled, circling the woman. "So she fucks them, then she *fucks* them. Very nice."

"Hmmm," Tabitha considered the woman for a moment, crossing her arms over her chest and tapping her boot clad foot against the ground. The others stepped up closer to her, examining her as someone would examine a rare animal at the zoo.

Look at the cute little serial killer. Oh look at her, she's so adorable. We just have-to-have her, Veronica heard them thinking, while she fought not to smirk at their logic. It was ironic really, the vampires had no problem killing innocent people, but when it came to serial killers, they needed to review their options!

Taking a few steps forward, Veronica stood at Tabitha's side. "You can't be seriously considering turning her?"

"She's not much to look at, skin and bones," Sebastian looked the woman, newly identified as the New England Mistress, up and down. His eyes lingered on her ample breasts, which nearly spilled out of the corset she happened to be wearing.

Tabitha dismissed his concern with a wave of her hand. "The woman's sick, what do you expect!" She began to walk around the dark haired woman, eyeing her intently. "You know it's funny. We vampires kill because it's in our nature. We are made to kill. Born to be predators."

Tabitha stood eye-to-eye with the woman, taking her chin in her hand. "You're a human and you love to kill, for the sake of killing. Like vampires, but not. It would be interesting to see what you'd be like as one of us."

"She's a god-damned lunatic, Tabitha!" Reaching out, Veronica caught Tabitha's upper arm in her hand, to gain her attention. "Kill her and get it over with!"

Jerking her arm from Veronica's grasp, Tabitha glared at her. "Don't forget who you're talking to."

Chyna jumped up and down, clapping her hands. "Yes, let's keep her."

The woman said nothing. Even her thoughts were abnormally quiet. Examining the woman, Veronica noticed a number of track marks littering her arms. Perhaps it was the drugs that kept her mind from being easily read? There was so much she still needed to learn about her new ability.

Reaching out, Veronica grasped the woman's wrist and extended her arm out for the others to see. "She's a heroin addict, in addition to being a serial killer! I don't mean any disrespect Tabitha, but I think this would be a bad idea. I don't think she would have any control over her thirst."

Their leader said nothing. Veronica could hear her weighing the pros and cons of adding this woman to their little family. The pros in her mind seemed to outweigh Veronica's objections.

Royally fucked up shit, Veronica thought. As far as she was concerned, this was a no brainer. This woman, an addict and serial killer was too much of a wild card to be turned. They already had enough crazy in the group as far as she was concerned.

If they don't kill her, I will, Veronica vowed. *One way or another, I'll kill her*.

Chapter 3

"What's going on?" Ricardo asked coming out of the adjoining restaurant and walking towards the store counter where Julie and Sandy stood watching the vampires across the parking lot.

"I think they're going to turn her," Julie responded, but didn't move her eyes away from the group outside.

"Damn it! Just want we need - another one!" Ricardo ran a shaky hand through his thick, black hair. He leaned back against the front of the counter and began to watch the scene in the parking lot unfold.

"She looks familiar..." Julie squinted, straining to see the woman's facial features.

"I was thinking the same thing," Sandy nodded in agreement. She paused for a moment. "Yes, I saw her on television the other day. She was on the news."

Pulling her eyes away from the happenings outside, Julie looked curiously at Sandy. "Why was she on the news?"

Sandy chewed on her bottom lip as she nervously played with a stray strand of blond hair that had escaped from her tightly bound ponytail.

The silence seemed to last an eternity as both Julie and Ricardo waited for her to come up with the desired information.

"She's a serial killer!" Sandy exclaimed, slapping the palm of her hand down on the counter, causing both Julie and Ricardo to jump back, startled. "The New England Mistress they call her. Or something like that. She's an HIV positive, heroin addicted prostitute that has been going around sleeping with unsuspecting men. Dozens of men have contracted the HIV virus from her so far."

"Wow," Julie shook her head slowly. She pulled out the silver cross she wore from under her blouse and rubbed the edges.

Normally, Julie wasn't a very devout catholic, but felt if there was ever a time to pray, this was the time. She didn't know enough about vampires yet to fully comprehend just how potentially disastrous the turning of the woman outside would be. Perhaps the virus died when the human turned?

"Veronica isn't like the others, she is rational," Julie stated, more to reassure herself than the others, "she will make the rest of them listen to reason."

The words had just left her mouth when Tabitha produced a knife and slit the prostitute's throat. Blood gushed from the wound as she collapsed to the ground. Julie's heart leapt into her throat. Maybe they were simply going to kill her and be done with it. The hope was short-lived. Sebastian stepped over the woman, straddling her. He bit into his wrist and placed it over her mouth.

I can't believe they're actually turning her. Julie shook her head in dismay.

"So now we have four 'normal' vampires and one serial killer vampire on our hands," tears began to stream down Sandy's cheeks, "what are we going to do?"

Ricardo shrugged, remaining silent.

Julie only shook her head.

A bad situation just got a number of times worse.

****

Veronica stood leaning against the wall of the new vampire's bedroom, watching her sleep. Tabitha had renamed her Scarlet once she was reborn. The new vampire, Scarlet, was every bit as vicious and unpredictable as Veronica had presumed she would be. Once the transformation had finished taking place she had woken up hungry and devoured the inhabitants of all six semi-trucks that were parked in the lot.

Scarlet's rampage forced them to dispose of the trucks and drivers. Not an easy thing to do. They had collided two of the trucks together on the highway, making it look like an accident. The other four trucks, *with* their trailers were currently lined up behind the old farmhouse the group currently inhabited. Tabitha swore she would take care of it. Veronica was curious to see how she planned on getting rid of them all, not to mention the remains of the rotting corpses they housed. They sure as hell couldn't remain on the property for much longer without being discovered.

She didn't even want to consider the smell that would inevitably drift to the house in a day or two.

The previous night Veronica had stood guard over the three humans inside the truck stop, with a tire iron in hand. She intended to use the tire iron as a stake if the new vampire dared come near them. Scarlet had devoured the inhabitants of the six trucks then collapsed to the ground exhausted from the turning and subsequent feeding frenzy.

Scarlet had left a bloody mess, which the rest of them were forced to clean up. Tabitha assured her that Scarlet would be made to understand their rules. That would be the end of the massacres; a single, isolated incident. Veronica highly doubted it. She dreaded the coming night. Could only imagine the problems Scarlet was going to cause. The only thing that was good about Scarlet was the fact that she made Chyna and Sebastian look like angels in comparison.

Pushing herself away from the wall, she walked closer to the sleeping vampire. She twirled a cast iron fireplace poker in her hand as if it were a baton, as she walked closer. Once she reached the side of the bed, she looked down at the vampire. Her looks had indeed improved since being turned. The track marks that had littered her arms were gone. Her body had reformed itself to a healthy weight, so her bones were no longer evident.

As for the disease, Tabitha informed them that the virus would have died with the death of her human body. In a sense, the New England Mistress was finally laid to rest.

While she would have figured Scarlet to have been in her late forties last night, looking down on her now, she would guess her human age to be roughly thirty. She now looked healthy, or at least as healthy as a vampire could look, Veronica supposed.

Veronica looked at the poker and then back to Scarlet. It would be so easy to simply stake her now. Have it over and done with. The only thing stopping her was the reaction of the others. As much as she disliked them, the truth was that for a while longer she needed them.

She needed them to educate her in the ways of the vampires. She also knew that if she were to leave, they would come after her. So for now she would stay and she would tolerate the new liability sleeping soundly below her, cuddled deep in the blankets of the luxurious king sized bed, as if she were royalty.

"Give me a reason, I beg you, and this will go straight through your heart," she promised as she pressed the point of the poker into Scarlet's chest, directly over her heart. "Just one good reason," she repeated.

Veronica heard footsteps coming from the hallway. Turning her head, but not removing the poker from Scarlet's chest, Veronica looked over to see who it was.

"What do you think you're doing Veronica?" Tabitha asked as she appeared in the doorway. Leaning against the door jamb, she crossed her arms over her chest.

Veronica tapped the new vampire in the chest with the poker several times before pulling it away. "Just visiting," she replied with a dry smile.

"She'll be a wonderful addition. You'll see." Tabitha looked down at Scarlet then back up to meet Veronica's eyes. "I suggest you learn to get along with her," she chuckled, giving Veronica a wink. "Forever is a long time to live with people you don't care for. Perhaps you should quit fighting what you now are." With that she turned on her heel and left Veronica alone with the sleeping Scarlet.

Forever *was* a long time, and Veronica had no intention of spending it with any of *them*. Things had just gotten a little more complicated for her that was all. She couldn't leave their little family until Scarlet was dead. Dead for good. She had a feeling Tabitha knew this. With Scarlet alive she was trapped with the group. She'd find a way to kill Scarlet. Maybe she'd think of a way to make it look like an accident? Of course, the problem was that it would be mighty hard to convince the others that Scarlet had accidently beheaded, drained or staked herself. She chuckled at the thought.

"I'll find a way," she vowed. Frustrated and hungry, Veronica turned on her heel and walked from the room, closing the door behind her.

****

Julie watched the sun as it lowered behind the mountain and felt the usual uneasiness she always felt this time of night. Only this time it was intensified twice over. Last night had been terrifying. The newest vampire had slaughtered the half dozen truckers in the lot. If it hadn't been for Veronica, she was quite certain she, Sandy and Ricardo would have also ended up on the menu.

While the other vampires scared her, the vampire they had decided to name Scarlet absolutely terrified her. So terrified, that she was almost able to break the hold they had on her and quit her job today. She came close, closer than she had even been able to before. She supposed with enough motivation and determination, she might be able to sever the hold once and for all.

Perhaps Sandy and Ricardo might also be able to do the same? New hope arose within her, despite the previous night's misfortunes. Julie reached behind her and fingered the cold metal of the steel stake she had secured under the waistband, at the back of her jeans. It would do nicely if it came to that tonight. She'd be damned if she would be some nutcase vampire's supper. Satisfied, she could reach it easily enough if need be, Julie pulled her t-shirt over the stake.

Looking over at the clock on her case register she noticed they were late. She almost let out a laugh when she thought of how annoyed Tabitha had been while cleaning up Scarlet's mess. They had been so busy with damage control that none of the vampires had eaten, with the exception of Scarlet.

No doubt they would be especially irritable tonight. To make matters worse the truck stop was busy than usual just now. There were a few truckers in the trucker's lounge, one taking a shower, and a number of people in the restaurant. If the vamps couldn't control their newest addition tonight there would be no way they would be able to cover their tracks two nights in a row.

At least another massacre would draw enough attention that we might be able to get rid of them once and for all. She shook her head at the thought. She wanted out of this mess; away from them and the truck stop from hell, but not at the expense of more innocent people.

A grey SUV drove up to the front of the store and three young men, college boys if she had to take a guess, hopped out. The driver, along with his passengers, looked intoxicated. She seriously doubted whether even one of the boys was of age. They stumbled to the entrance, each one leaning on the other for support.

Looking past them, and across the interstate, she noticed Chyna emerge from the woods.

On normal nights, if it was busy, the vampires would hold back until it slowed enough that they could be discreet. As Scarlet emerged from the woods, followed by Tabitha, she had a feeling this wasn't going to be a normal night.

"You grab some Coke, I gotta go take-a piss," the driver of the SUV yelled to his two companions, despite them being only a few feet away from him.

"Yah," the youngest one replied making his way to the back of the store, towards the coolers.

The third one, a red-headed young man she guessed to be twenty or twenty-one, headed for the snack foods section.

All five of the vampires were now across the interstate and making their way towards the store. Scarlet was now leading the way. *Nothing like an overzealous vampire to start the night off right*, Julie thought.

As usual, Veronica was trailing behind the group. Her eyes were fixated on Scarlet. The expression Veronica was wearing on her face reminded Julie of a mother who was watching her ill-behaved child, just waiting for it to do something bad. The look was a combination of dread and anger. No, anger wasn't the correct word, it was more than that. It was a look of pure hatred.

Hmm, now that's an interesting development. She began to wonder how the rest of the clan were making out with their newest family member.

She fingered the stake at her back once more. She could feel it pressed hard against her back, but her fingers having contact with it seemed to give her an added sense of security.

"Come on jackass, we got what we need," the red headed college boy yelled into the men's room. He then turned and made his way, half-stumbling, half-walking, to the cash counter.

The youngest of the three came behind him with a six can pack of Coca-Cola. They laid out their purchases consisting of Coke, and an armload of junk food on the counter.

"Look at what's coming this way." The red-haired one said letting out a low whistle. He leaned his back against the counter, his arms crossed over his chest and watched as the vamps made their way across the parking lot.

"Mmm-hmm. *Love* the jugs on that little sweetheart." The driver had returned from the restroom and was now leaning against the counter beside the red-haired passenger, also openly admiring Tabitha.

The vampires piled into the store. Several of the customers in the restaurant turned and stared, wide-eyed. They, however, were smart enough to look away once they realized their stares were being noticed.

"That'll be twenty-four sixty-seven boys," Julie said as she began to quickly bag up their purchases. She hoped that she could get them out without incident. It was a long shot, but she had to try. *At least they're so drunk they wouldn't need to have their mind screwed with after the feeding*, Julie mused. She would have laughed at her little silent joke if it wasn't such a heinous topic to joke about.

The vampires surrounded the college boys, all eyeing each of the young men with slight grins on their faces. Tabitha, however, was the one who approached them. Her step was so graceful, she appeared to be gliding. She tilted her head to the left, her black eyes locking onto each of theirs. She took another step closer, so that barely an inch separated them.

The murmur of voices that were coming from the restaurant became silent. The boys became silent. Despite their drunken state they seemed to feel the tension in the room. It was as if everyone was waiting to see what she would do, and hear how the boys would respond.

Tabitha lowered her face to the driver's neck. She inhaled, taking in his scent. When she lifted her head, her dark eyes had turned, blood red. "So you like these do you?" She asked trailing her fingers over her breasts in much the same way as you might display a prize up for grabs.

He nodded. "Very nice," he replied in a weak voice as he licked his lips. A dopey grin spread across his face. He didn't seem to notice her sudden change in eye colour, or the appearance of her fangs. He didn't notice since his eyes seemed to be drawn to, and didn't sway from, her breasts under the tight fitting black tank top.

"Then come with me," she pivoted around and began to walk from the store, swaying her hips seductively. All eyes in the place were glued to her and the young man, as if everyone seemed to sense something bad was about to happen. The driver of the SUV trotted off behind her, as though he were a lost puppy who had just found his owner.

She led him out of view from the store window, leaving Julie with the remaining vampires and two college guys. With Tabitha out of sight, Scarlet seemed to get increasingly anxious.

Julie noticed a remarkable difference in Scarlett's appearance from the previous night. The previous night she looked sickly, near death, while still alive. Tonight, the second night of her undead life, she looked more healthy and alive then she had before she died. To look more alive dead, than you did when you were alive seemed deeply ironic to Julie.

Scarlet also looked hungry. The way she was looking at the two remaining college boys made Julie feel more scared than she'd ever been before. She looked feral, savage, untamed. She looked at the boys, the red-headed one in particular, like a drug addict looked at their next shot of heroine. *Blood the drug of choice when you're a vampire*, Julie mused.

In Julie's eyes, the boys' chances of getting to their destination had just lowered substantially.

She ventured a glance at Veronica, who had her eyes glued on Scarlet. It was painfully apparent she didn't like the newcomer and was waiting for a chance to end Scarlet's life. Julie reached back and fingered the stake under her shirt once again. That made two of them.

Maybe if she just got them outside and into their car, they'd make it to wherever they were headed? Maybe she had an ally in Veronica? Perhaps if they worked together they could end Scarlet and the rest of the clan's lives for good? Julie caught Veronica's eyes and a strange sort of knowledge passed between them. An understanding.

"Twenty-four, sixty-seven," Julie repeated snapping her fingers in front of the red-head's eyes, which seemed to break the trance he was in. He glanced quickly at the faces of the four remaining vampires, before proceeding to dig his wallet out of the pocket of his trousers. He fumbled when opening his wallet, but finally managed to pull out a couple of crisp twenty dollar bills and pass them to her.

Chyna strode up to the red-headed one, as Julie was passing him his change. "I've always liked men with red hair. It's so," she thought for a moment, as if trying to come up with just the right word, "alive." She trailed a finger down his bare arm as she spoke.

Scarlet followed Chyna's lead approaching the third of the college boys. "We can show you things, *do things* to you that you could only dream about," she purred.

Sebastian grunted, bored with what was transpiring in front of him and made his way into the restaurant and out of sight.

Julie thrust the change at the red-headed college kid. "Have a good evening." She hoped he'd take the hint, but the look he was giving Chyna at that moment said there was no chance in that.

A scream filled the air surrounding the truck stop. The scream was dripping with utter terror. A second scream came directly afterwards, followed by silence. The patrons of the restaurant and in the truckers' lounge all sat up straight in their seats, their ears perked, listening for another scream. When it never came, the silence was broken as conversations in hushed voices began.

"Kevin!" the red-haired guy exclaimed. He made an attempt to make a run for the door, but was stopped as Chyna's hand gripped his upper arm. Her fingernails dug into his pale cream-coloured flesh. Seconds later, a thin stream of blood seeped from the wounds.

"Where are *you* running off to, cowboy?" Chyna purred.

"You crazy bitch, let go of me!" He tried to jerk his arm free, but her grasp held tight.

Chyna laughed.

Scarlet laughed.

"I demand to know where Kevin is and I want to know now!" His face had grown nearly as red as his hair as his temper rose. He stood looking down at Chyna towering over her by several inches.

"Who are you people? What do you *want*?" The third one asked. He looked from vampire to vampire. His gaze landed on Veronica. "What is wrong with your crazy-assed friends?"

Veronica shook her head in response.

"Red!" the red-haired guy screamed. "Look at their eyes! When did they become red? What the..."

A couple who had been dining in the restaurant scurried out of the store. Once outside, they took a brief look back at the group in front of the cash register and broke into a run making their way towards their truck.

Chyna stared deep into the red-haired student's eyes. "Nothing's going on here. Your friend is getting laid; having the time of his life. You want to join him?"

The red-haired one nodded in agreement, "Lucky bastard. Bet he's getting his dick sucked right this second. Everything is great."

"What? Mike?" The third student looked at the red-headed one, Mike, with a bewildered look on his face. "What are you talking about? What's going on?" He looked from vampire to vampire once again.

Chyna stepped up to the third student looking deep into his eyes and then said: "Your buddy is fine. In fact, you want to stroll behind the store here and check things out. It's all good here."

He nodded and let out a little laugh, then shrugged. "Yah, you're right. It's all good here."

"Let's *all* go find your friend," Chyna looked over at Scarlet who grinned and winked.

Both college boys nodded.

"Good, then follow me," Chyna instructed making her way across the store and out the front door with Scarlet and the two young men in tow.

Scarlet turned back to glare at Veronica. "You coming?"

"No," came Veronica's curt reply as she glared at the newest vampire.

"You know, Veronica, I'm here to stay. Get used to it," Scarlet smiled a wickedly, sadistic smile. Her red eyes blazed. Turning on her heel, she walked out of the door and quickly disappeared from view.

Several minutes later there were a couple more sets of screams. Blood-curdling, anguished screams. Several people from the restaurant and a couple from the truckers' lounge scurried out of the store and into their respective vehicles. They didn't waste any time driving out of the truck stop and onto the interstate.

Julie closed her eyes, trying to block out the sounds. When she opened her eyes she noticed Veronica's deep green eyes eyeing her intently.

"Keep strong," Veronica leaned over the counter and whispered into Julie's ear before turning and leaving the store, walking in the direction of the numerous parked semi-trucks.

Chapter 4

"Coming," Veronica yelled as she made her way to the front door of the old farmhouse she and the others inhabited. The front porch was specially designed to allow the vampires to go onto it without fear of being scorched by the sun. All the windows had a UV blocking filter to allow the sunshine without the pain.

She looked at the grandfather clock in the living room. It was noon. All the others were sleeping soundly from the feast they had indulged in last night. The vampires, Tabitha, Chyna and Scarlet had drained the three college students, thrown them all back into the SUV, driven the vehicle into a nearby lake and pushed it in with the dead bodies inside it. They had watched it sink to the bottom, just as the sun was beginning its ascent over the horizon.

The knocking continued, louder and more aggressive now. Veronica sighed as she opened the door to reveal two police officers, both with stern looks on their faces. One was a young, handsome man who looked to be just out of the academy. The other was an older, presumably more seasoned officer, with dark hair speckled with silver and possessing piercing grey eyes.

"Could we come in? We have some questions concerning the trucks parked out back," the older officer started. Not waiting for a reply he pushed past Veronica. The younger officer hesitated then followed his partner into the farmhouse.

Great, just great, Veronica thought with a sigh, closing the door behind them.

"So you're um..." the officer appeared to be looking down at a piece of paper attached to a clipboard he had brought with him, "Mrs. Evans? Is Mr. Evans here as well? We'd like to speak with him also," the older officer stated while looking over his surroundings.

Mr. Evans? Mrs. Evans? She thought for a moment before realizing that would have been the names of the previous owners. Their names would still be stencilled on the mailbox no doubt. The owners, whose carcasses were now worm food out in the back garden.

Veronica smiled sweetly at him, extending her hand, "Yes, I'm Mrs. Evans. I'm afraid Mr. Evans is away at the moment."

The officer nodded, "Could you show me some identification, Mrs. Evans?"

I think if given the opportunity I could give that little piece-of-ass a go, the older officer's thoughts rang into her head, *Maybe the trucker isn't lost after all. But that wouldn't explain the other three trucks. Perhaps we should have called for backup.*

Four trucks out back: this could be big, the younger officer's thoughts cut in. *Just look at the way Rider is eyeing the suspect. Course he's old, but not dead - who could blame him?*

"You alright miss?" the younger officer asked, turning to face her. He reached towards his hip, towards his gun.

Hmmm. I smell humans. Breakfast in bed perhaps? One of the vamps had just awoken and Veronica tuned into her thoughts. She guessed it was Scarlet. She needed to get the cops out of here now, before a bad situation became infinitely worse.

Veronica sensed that the older officer would be easier to compel, so started with him. Placing a hand on his forearm she looked deeply into his eyes. He gave her an odd, surprised look, but didn't attempt to pull away.

"You didn't see any semi-trucks here. You met Mrs *and* Mr Evans. They invited you in for tea, which you declined. Everything is great here. No problems, no concerns. You won't need to come back," Veronica told him, feeding the information directly into his mind.

He promptly turned to his partner, "All's fine here; let's go."

The younger officer pulled his gun, aiming it at Veronica's chest. "Step back and put your hands where I can see them, Mrs. Evans."

Before she had a chance to react, Scarlet appeared behind the younger officer. She snarled, her eyes turning, fangs dropping. Coming up from behind him she grabbed onto his arms, pulling them tightly behind his back. He grunted, dropping the gun, which made a clunking noise as it hit the floor. As she lowered her head to sink her fangs into the shocked officer's neck, Veronica moved into action.

She gave Scarlet a forceful shove, which sent her falling backwards to land hard against the kitchen wall. Her eyes narrowed as she snarled at Veronica.

"You kill them, we'll all be hunted. You're the reason they're here to begin with," Veronica snapped, glaring at the new vampire.

"Wha...what? What *are* you?" The younger officer sputtered.

The older, seasoned officer didn't react, but simply stood in place as if waiting for his next command. Veronica gripped both of the younger officer's upper arms in her hands, looked deeply into his eyes then spoke the same words to him that she had to his partner.

The younger officer nodded. "Nothing suspicious here, we're sorry to have wasted your time, Mrs. Evans. Come on, Rider. There's nothing here."

Officer Rider nodded tipping his hat to her and Scarlet, "Good day, ladies."

Veronica and Scarlet watched from the window above the kitchen sink as the officers left the house. They watched them slide into their patrol car and drive slowly back down the long dirt driveway. Seconds later the car disappeared out of sight.

With the threat gone, Veronica turned to Scarlet, enraged. "What did you think you were doing?" She demanded, jabbing a finger into Scarlet's chest.

Scarlet's red eyes met Veronica's green ones. "Doing what was necessary."

"*I* did what was necessary. *I* had the situation under control." With her emotions rising, her eyes shifted from green to red and her body began to vibrate as the hatred intensified. "Even Chyna wouldn't have pulled a stupid stunt like that!"

Scarlet threw her head back and laughed. Her shrill laughter filled the small country kitchen. "Yes, you had it all under control. That's why you had a gun pointed at your chest. I would think a 'thank you' would be in order here."

Taking a deep breath Veronica shook her head. Her eyes slipped back to green. "The gun wouldn't have killed me. You know that." She took another deep breath, as she leaned against the kitchen counter. "You just can't see the big picture can you? There is a *reason* why vampires live in a world of secrecy; a *reason* why we don't allow our presence to be known to humans."

Scarlet took a step closer to Veronica, her eyes gleaming. "We shouldn't *have* to hide. We are stronger, faster, better than humans, in every way. The only thing they are good for is food. We can take over. We can have them worshipping at our feet if we choose. So why *do* we choose to hide?" Scarlet's eyes narrowed. "*I* won't hide," she hissed through clenched teeth.

Veronica pushed herself off the counter to stand just inches away from the taller Scarlet. "Then I will kill you myself. And this time you'll stay dead," she promised, pausing for a moment to ensure her threat sank in, then brushed past Scarlet, heading for the staircase.

You're welcome to try, Scarlet's thoughts echoed in Veronica's mind as she headed up the winding staircase to the upper storey bedrooms. She would have to act soon before Scarlet either developed a power that would hamper her chances of killing her, or worse still, she did something that would expose them all.

She didn't want to imagine what could happen if humans got a whiff of the fact vampires were among them. The humans' fear of vampires would lead to hatred and paranoia. With fear and paranoia it wouldn't be a very big jump to consider large armies of humans seeking out their kind, exterminating them out of existence. It would be like a modern day witch hunt.

While there were a good many vampires she assumed to be like Scarlet and the others in her new 'family'- nasty, hateful and vindictive - she wouldn't mind betting there were also a good many like her. Just trying to survive the best way they could; trying not to hurt anyone, just wanting to live out their immortal lives. Those would be the vampires who would suffer the most. Those would be the ones likely to be murdered by the hunters. Or worse.

****

Over the next several nights Julie noticed a definite increase in tension between Scarlet and Veronica, if that were even possible at this point. They would glower at each other, make snide comments, and on one particular evening they had nearly come to blows. Tabitha had stepped between them, scolding them both for acting like rival siblings, which Julie supposed in a distorted, fucked-up kind of way they were.

While Tabitha became annoyed with the two vampires, and had to spend the majority of her time at the truck stop playing referee, Chyna seemed to simply enjoy the added conflict. Julie could tell she was doing everything in her power to fuel the animosity between the two. Just like she was doing currently.

"So what's the deal with Ricardo anyhow?" Scarlet asked as she lounged against the store's front counter.

"Just leave the staff here alone Scarlet," Veronica said. She was standing next to the store's large front window looking out but took a moment to turn and shoot Scarlet a disgusted look. She then transferred her attention back to the darkened parking lot. It was well past midnight, on a moonless night. There wasn't much to see from what Julie could tell, but it seemed that Veronica was intent on something.

Julie had no idea where Sebastian and Tabitha were tonight. For some odd reason they hadn't shown up with the other three. It was the first time since they had started appearing that they hadn't all come together as a group. Maybe things were changing within the vampire clan? Julie reached behind her and fingered the silver stake she now carried with her each night. Ricardo also carried one with him every night. Because of Sebastian's insistence of having close physical contact with Sandy she couldn't risk keeping one on her, instead she kept one in a drawer under the cash register, not the most ideal place, but better than nothing.

Chyna, who was perched on the counter, her long slender legs crossed, gave Julie a jab in the ribs with her elbow. Julie looked up and received a wicked smile, a smile that told her that shit was about to hit the fan if Chyna had anything to do with it. "I think Veronica over there has a soft spot for Ricardo. I dare you to make a move on him."

Veronica spun around to face them, glaring from Chyna's smug, smiling face to Scarlet standing close to her, with her own devilishly sadistic look.

"Have you taken a fancy to our dear little Ricardo in the restaurant, Veronica?" Scarlet asked, her red painted lips smiled, showing a gleaming set of vampire fangs. She glanced quickly at Chyna who kept a smirk on her face, anxious to see a fight commence. "He does look like he'd be nice and ripe."

"Go get Ricardo," Scarlet turned to Julie, demanding.

Julie hesitated, looking from vampire to vampire. If she did what Scarlet wanted and set off to fetch Ricardo from the restaurant then there was no doubt Scarlet would feed off him, if for no other reason than to prove a point to Veronica. Scarlet was watching Veronica with hatred in her eyes, her expression dared the other vampire to try and stop her.

Julie reached behind her and fingered the stake tucked into the waistband of her jeans. *If only Scarlet could be distracted enough for me to stake her,* Julie thought. The vampires were abnormally fast, but if she was distracted then perhaps the element of surprise would be on her side. As if sensing what she was contemplating Veronica caught Julie's eyes and shook her head mouthing the word: *No.*

"Fine. I'll go get him," Chyna slid off the counter and strutted her way over to the restaurant, disappearing around the corner.

"The humans are not to be touched. Those are Tabitha's rules, unless you've been granted permission." Veronica stated, shifting her attention back to Scarlet.

"Funny, I don't seem to see her or Sebastian here at the moment. Guess that means we're rules-free for the night," came the retort from Scarlet.

"They're not here because they're cleaning up *your* mess. You *do* remember the four semi-trucks and trailers that still have to be disposed of, don't you? I'd have killed you that night if I'd been Tabitha."

A car pulled up directly in front of the store entrance. A middle aged couple exited the black luxury sedan, heading for the convenience store. Julie looked at the digital clock on the cash register it flashed three-seventeen am in bright red numbers. *Don't tourists ever consider motels at night anymore?*

She watched Scarlet's eyes light up as the couple entered the store. They were arguing as they walked, not seeming to notice the two vampires, eyes red, fangs bared. They walked by Veronica without giving her a second glance.

"Well if you'd taken the turnoff like I asked you to, then we would have been *there* by now," the woman, Julie presumed to be the wife, bitched at her husband.

"God! I'm so sick of listening to your mouth, Beth, so sick. To hell with it, maybe we should just turn around and go home? Screw the wedding," the husband shot back, his voice rising slightly with each word spoken.

"I'm going to the bathroom. Ask directions," the wife instructed as she wandered off in the direction of the washrooms.

The husband, a tall, lean fellow with thick brown hair showing a tiny hint of grey running through it around the temples, ran a shaky hand through his tousled mane. He shook his head at the floor before trudging his way over to the counter Julie was standing behind. Scarlet shifted positions so she was now leaning provocatively against it.

"Hey stranger, you lost?" she purred as he reached the counter. She jutted out her chest, clad in a red velvet corset. Julie had noticed over the past number of days it seemed that corsets and short skirts were the only clothing the new vampire possessed. Her breasts nearly spilled over the bodice. Looking at Scarlet, Julie supposed old habits must die hard.

"Yah, we made a wrong turn somewhere. I think we missed the exit..." The man murmured not paying much attention to Scarlet.

"Maybe I can be of assistance?" she continued, reaching out to trail a finger down his chest.

Veronica seeming to notice that trouble could just be minutes away and stepped up beside Scarlet, their recent argument put on hold for the time being.

Her touch, which Julie knew from experience would be cool and silky, attracted the man's attention. He looked Scarlet over, slowly working his gaze up the length of her slim, but shapely legs, over her hips and flat stomach, pausing at her ample breasts then on up to her ruby red lips, which she evidently noticed him staring at, as she slowly ran her tongue over them leaving them shining and inviting.

Once he reached her eyes he let out a quick gasp and took a half step back. He then seemed to relax again and let out a little chuckle. "Contact lenses right? Going to some type of rave party?"

Scarlet considered it for a moment, before closing the distance between them. "What if I told you I was a vampire?" She placed one palm flat on his blue polo shirt clad chest while the other snaked it way under the material to feel the warm flesh beneath.

"I...um..." he paused for a moment, shifting from one foot to another uncomfortably.

"Reggie!" A harsh female voice screeched from behind the group.

"Beth!" The sound of her voice seemed to break the trance, which momentarily had him caught up. He quickly stepped away from Scarlet, nearly stumbling over his own feet. A look of guilt passed over his face as it reddened several shades. He hung his head, seeming to find something interesting on the spot of the floor between his feet.

Scarlet let her hands drop to her sides, her lips formed a pout. She took a step back and leaned against the counter once again, watching his wife as she stormed over to them, her face distorted with rage.

Beth planted herself firmly in front of Scarlet and glared at her. They were nearly eye to eye but Beth had a slight height advantage, and at least fifty pounds of excess weight. "You hussy!" she shrieked. "Can't you see he's married?" She reached out and snatched up her husband's left hand, raising it to Scarlet's eye level as she pointed at the ring. "He's *taken*."

Julie gasped and took a step away from the counter. The poor woman had no idea what she was about to get herself into. Julie reached back and fingered the stake, extra reassurance it was still there in case she was forced to do what was necessary. Or at least attempt to.

The vampires had already gone out to feed off the truckers earlier that evening so they certainly didn't need to feed from the tourists. Scarlet had proven, on numerous occasions, both as a human and even more now as a vampire, that she had no regard for human life.

Wrong place, wrong time, Julie mused. She looked over at Veronica, but Veronica wasn't paying any attention to her. Her gaze was busy jumping between the two potential combatants.

Scarlet threw her head back and laughed. This seemed to anger the woman more, but she said nothing. Once the laughter subsided she fixed her eyes on Beth, meeting her gaze. She stepped so close to the woman, they were almost touching. They were a mere fraction of an inch apart. She sniffed the side of Beth's neck, her fangs bared as the husband looked on in stunned silence.

"Perhaps, you're just jealous my interest isn't in you, huh?" She whispered in the woman's ear before lowering her head to nibble on the nape of her neck. The woman's husband, Reggie, looked on with an expression that contained a mixture of shock and arousal.

The woman quieted down, partially stunned, partially compelled. It appeared she was beginning to get the idea that her big mouth, might have gotten her in over her head. Perhaps her subconscious was screaming danger to her that very second, causing her body to freeze in anticipation.

Why isn't Veronica stopping this? Julie glanced over at Veronica and noticed she had her head cocked to the side, as if listening for something. Her red eyes seemed to be vacant, in a daze.

The thoughts of those around her, anxious and fast-paced bombarded Veronica's mind, crashing through her skull like a semi truck:

Julie: *Is she reading their minds?*

Scarlet: *One taste, just one taste.*

Reggie: *Not sure if I should be scared for our lives or horny as hell.*

Beth: *Her breath feels like ice. Am I going to die? What is she? I don't want to die! Please God! Reggie! Do something.*

Scarlet: *Hmmm, maybe I can indulge in a combo meal. They won't be missed.*

Julie: *Why isn't she doing anything?*

Reggie: *Shit I am horny! There's got to be something wrong with me.*

Chyna, re-entering the room: *What the hell is going on in here?*

Ricardo, entering the store from the restaurant, directly behind Chyna: *I'll stake her before I let that vamp whore drink from me.*

Scarlet: *One taste*.

Julie: *Veronica, DO something*!

Scarlet urged Beth's head to her shoulder, exposing the soft creamy flesh on the opposite side. She pulled Beth close to her. Opening her mouth, fangs bared she lowered her mouth to the woman's neck, piercing the skin.

Beth let out a terrified scream, but her scream was cut off by the sound of an explosion; an explosion so loud that it shook the truck stop right down to its foundation. Scarlet's head jerked up from her feast and peered out of the large front window. In fact, all heads left the horrific sight of Beth being drained right there in the middle of the convenience store and spun in the direction of the window.

The group, vampires and humans alike, quickly ran outside into the parking lot searching for the source of the boom. Looking to the North, Julie's mouth fell open. A large mushroom of black, grey and orange smoke rose up into the air a mile or so away, just visible in the night sky. The faint smell of burning diesel drifted towards them moments later.

"My god," Julie gasped.

The sound of Julie's voice seemed to bring everyone's attention back to their current surroundings. Behind her Julie heard a car starting and, turning, she saw that Reggie and Beth had taken the opportunity to jump into their car and make a hasty getaway.

The tires of their sedan squealed as Reggie shifted it into drive and shot out of the parking lot, cutting off an oncoming SUV as it came barrelling down the interstate. The vehicle was heading north, in the direction of the explosion. The SUV's horn blared, angrily at the sedan. The driver of the SUV swerved to avoid rear-ending it. The speed, in addition to the severity of the swerve, caused the SUV to nearly roll, the tires on the right hand side of the vehicle lifted for a split second from the asphalt before settling back down to the ground. With some difficulty, but with luck and skilful manoeuvring, the driver of the SUV finally got the truck back under control and continued driving in the direction it was heading.

"Wicked," Chyna commented smiling, as she pulled a Jolly Pop from the pocket of her brown bomber jacket. Pulling the wrapper off the candy, she discarded the wrapper on the ground and popped the strawberry Jolly Pop into her mouth.

There was silence for another minute as the group considered the collision and the mushroom cloud of smoke on the horizon. Several of the truckers had been roused by the commotion and were now standing by their trucks, looking on in awe.

"Guess that's what they call the one that got away," Scarlet remarked with a laugh.

Chyna looked over at Scarlet, laughing with her, that high pitched banshee laugh that grated so badly on Julie's nerves, before commenting, "Maybe they're playing hard to get?"

Scarlet wiped a dribble of blood from the side of her mouth with her index finger, then licked it off her finger, "It's just as well, the bitch tasted like grease and smelt like garlic, it was like sucking on a chicken leg from Chicken Shack's fried chicken menu."

Chyna broke out into a fit of laughter as she walked over to Scarlet and draped an arm over her shoulders. "I know just what you can use to wash it down with." She nodded towards Ricardo who was standing next to Julie, close to the store entrance. She lowered her lips to Scarlet's ear and whispered in her ear, "I fetched him for you."

Julie didn't care for the way Chyna and Scarlet were now focusing their attention on Ricardo. Sandy had already scurried back into the restaurant. Out of sight, out of mind.

Looking over at the parking area, she noticed that the truckers who had come out to see what the ruckus was about had gone back into their trucks. All the lights had been turned out in the cabs.

Julie chanced a hesitant look over at Veronica, hoping she would step forward and block the other vampire, but she didn't. Scarlet and Chyna closed the distance between them quickly. Scarlet's hips moved seductively as she sauntered toward Ricardo.

Scarlet stopped just inches from Ricardo, her eyes taking in every inch of him. She reached out and ran the back of her hand across his cheek. "I've always loved Latino men."

Ricardo glared down at her, he stood close to six feet tell, nearly six inches taller than her. "Lucky me."

Running her fingers across his shoulders she leaned into him breathing in deeply. "Smells so sweet," she turned back to Chyna, "I can't believe none of you have sampled from him yet. He's delightful."

Stepping up to Ricardo, Chyna also leaned in, breathing in his scent just as Scarlet had. "Mmmm, you're right." She took a step back, and crossed her arms over her chest pouting, "But Tabitha says he's off limits."

A wide, devious grin formed on Scarlet's face. "But *she's not here,* is she?"

Having seen enough and fearing for Ricardo, Julie placed herself between him and Scarlet. "I can't let you do this," Julie announced. She stood eye to eye with the vampire, defiantly.

Knowing how relentless Scarlet was with feeding, she didn't have much faith in Scarlet's willpower to stop once she had tasted him.

Julie took one last look at Veronica who seemed to be in a trance and dismissed any hope of getting assistance from the one she had considered to be her ally. Reaching behind her she fingered the silver stake at her back and decided it was time to take action.

Chapter 5

"Julie. No. I can fight my own battles," Ricardo protested, attempting to push her behind him and out of harm's way.

"Look who's developed a backbone," Chyna taunted, giggling.

Julie looked at Chyna briefly out of the corner of her eye, but her main interest was on Scarlet. Come hell or high water, she was not going to stand by and allow him to be drained by this psychopathic vampire.

This ends tonight, she vowed silently as she slowly slipped her right hand behind her and grasped the stake tightly. She would need to be fast. With the element of surprise on her side she just might have a shot.

"Move out of the way, or take his place," Scarlet snarled, her fangs bared.

"Move, Julie," Ricardo tried to step out from behind her, but she refused to let him.

"No," Julie met Scarlet's gaze with one of her own, challenging the vampire. "You want him, you need to go through me, you heroin-addicted whore."

There was silence for a brief moment, then without another word Scarlet lunged for Julie. She hit her with enough force to send them both tumbling to the ground. As she fell, Julie unsheathed the stake she had been concealing for the last week and raised it over her head. As luck would have it, when they both hit the cold ground Julie had landed on top. With as much force as she could muster, she drove the stake into Scarlet's chest. The vampire shrieked in agony, clawing at the silver stake protruding from her body.

"Get it out! Get it out!" she wailed, continuing to claw at her chest, ripping the material of her bodice and gashing deep cuts into herself in the process. Her body bucked and jerked under Julie, but she wouldn't die. She simply continued to scream and claw at her chest.

Realizing that she hadn't quite gotten the heart like she had planned, Julie reached for the stake hoping to reposition it in an attempt to puncture her heart, when she felt something hit her in the ribs. The force was so strong that it threw her off Scarlet and propelled her several yards away. She closed her eyes as she flew through the night air, landing against the ice machine. A pain shot through her entire body making her cry out.

"Just a tip you little cunt, if you're going to stake someone in the heart, get it right the first time." The pain from her side was intense, so intense she was uncertain who had actually said the words to her. All she was aware of was the feel of the cold body covering hers, and then the pinch as fangs broke the skin of her neck. A small trail of warm liquid slid down her neck, into her cleavage and onto the collar of her blouse. *Blood is such a bugger to remove from clothing*, she thought then laughed. Her laughter sounded hopeless, hollow.

She struggled, kicking out, beating her fists against the chest of her attacker, but it was no use. She was going to die, in the parking lot of the Night and Day Truck stop, the place where if you buy ten slushies, you get one free. She would die slumped against an ice machine.

Panic rose in her as she began to drift into unconsciousness. *Rats. Will the rats chew at my bleeding, dead carcass? Please Sandy or someone don't let the rats get me...*

"Don't want to die," she murmured in a voice barely louder than a whisper. She faded out completely realizing that death wouldn't be the worst option. What if they turned her? A fate worse than death indeed. A teardrop shimmered as it slid down her cheek and the world went black around her.

****

Tonight had turned out to be an opportunity for Veronica.

Scarlet had her mind set on sampling the Latino cuisine from the restaurant, despite Tabitha's instructions that the three workers of the truck stop were not to be fed from. Sebastian fed from Sandy, they all knew that. They also all knew he took more than blood from her, they just pretended they didn't. Tabitha had a soft spot for Sebastian, however; they'd been companions for a long, long time, so he indulged in little luxuries that were forbidden to the others.

As Veronica saw it, she was taking a gamble on the humans' lives. However, in the end, with Scarlet and Chyna lurking around, their life spans were not looking all that great at the moment, anyhow. If Tabitha decided it was time to move on, the three humans who worked at the Night and Day Truck Stop were as good as dead. She'd heard the thoughts of the others in regards to that topic. Sebastian would have his fun with Sandy, unlike anything she'd ever imagined in her wildest nightmares. Chyna had been itching for Julie's blood since they had first arrived at the truck stop and, of course, Scarlet would devour Ricardo.

That was the reality of the situation.

Julie and Ricardo had been keeping a stake on them, tucked away in the waistband of their pants for some time now. She didn't need to be able to read their minds to realize that. The humans were lucky the other vamps were more interested in feeding and causing trouble, than in actually watch the humans very closely.

Those you least expect to have the power to destroy you, quite frequently are the ones to see to your demise, Veronica thought.

She had hoped Julie wouldn't step in between Scarlet and Ricardo. She was anticipating Ricardo, staking Scarlet himself as she lunged at him to feed. Julie getting in the middle ruined that plan, but she had still held hope that Julie would aim well and perhaps get lucky.

She didn't. That much was clear as she was sent soaring several feet in the air, her body finally colliding with the ice machine.

There was still hope, and it was currently en route, which was why Veronica still stood rooted to her spot. She stood there listening, hearing, thinking.

While the others might not have realized this, there was a connection between Tabitha and Sebastian's absence and the explosion. They hadn't mentioned to the others, but once the rest had left for their nightly Night and Day hunting trip, Tabitha and Sebastian had taken two of the transport trucks out of the backyard and driven them up the 1-95 heading north, travelling in the opposite direction of the other two trucks they had crashed last week, which had been south of the truck stop. The explosion everyone had heard had been the trucks. They had gotten rid of two more pieces of evidence, which left two final trucks, both with rotting corpses inside, at the farmhouse.

Tabitha, especially, had been furious earlier that evening, back at the farmhouse. She was going to be missing the fun of feeding at the truck stop to clean up Scarlet's mess yet again; which was why taking action tonight was so critical. If Scarlet had been killed tonight by one of the humans then Tabitha might not have been too enraged. However, as things looked now, Tabitha would be there in time to witness Scarlet feeding on Julie. There to witness Scarlet openly defying yet another of her rules. That might be enough for her to consider allowing Veronica to kill Scarlett then and there. That was, if she didn't do it herself.

Tabitha and Sebastian were moving fast, within a minute they would be clearing the parking lot. She could faintly hear their thoughts and, as anticipated, Tabitha was pissed off and starving.

She listened to Julie's thoughts as the vampire drained her. She was still conscious; she was concerned about the stain the blood was making. Her heart rate was still strong, accelerated.

Tabitha and Sebastian: the cavalry. She would have laughed at the thought of them being considered cavalry if she wasn't so terrified they wouldn't get there in time. She fixed her gaze on Julie and Scarlet, bracing herself to tackle Scarlet at the last second if needed.

Rats, Don't let the rats..., Julie's thought's cried out in Veronica's head. Her heart rate was now slowing. She'd be dead in less than a minute.

Closer and closer. Their thoughts were clear now.

Don't want to die, Julie thoughts pleaded with Veronica.

As Julie sank into unconsciousness, Tabitha and Sebastian appeared. Within seconds Tabitha had tackled Scarlet, sending them both flying through the convenience store's large plate glass window. There was a crash, the sound of glass breaking as they fell through. As Chyna made a move to assist Scarlet, Sebastian stopped her, blocking her path.

Veronica shot into action, running over to Julie and falling to her knees at the human's side. She applied pressure to the wound to help stop the bleeding. Vampire bite marks healed quickly.

Veronica prayed Julie could hold on until then. Her heartbeat was faint to Veronica's ears, but still present.

She had no doubt Julie was going to hate her, maybe even more than she hated the others. Julie had trusted her and she had let her down. If her plan succeeded as she thought it might, perhaps Julie would understand. Perhaps... *You allowed a psychopathic vampire to nearly kill her! Sure she'll forgive that*, a voice in the back of her head sneered.

A vicious hiss brought Veronica's attention to Tabitha and Scarlet. They were inside the convenience store now. There was glass everywhere. It was going to be a bitch for the humans to clean up. Several large shards of glass hung ominously from the top of the window frame.

The hiss came from Scarlet. She was hunched over in attack mode, facing Tabitha. She reminded Veronica of a wild cat, cornered and ready to lash out; fangs bared, eyes a deep blood red. Tabitha stood roughly seven or eight feet away from her, her head high and shoulders back, glowering down at the newest vampire.

"The humans are forbidden," Tabitha shouted, anger flashing in her red eyes. "I've already had to spend the evening cleaning up your mistakes, now you've left me with another!"

Scarlet laughed - a wicked, blood-curdling laugh. "Then perhaps you should have a word with your precious Sebastian. He's had his fair share of sampling."

Tabitha quickly shot a glance at Sebastian as he tentatively stepped through the window to stand at Tabitha's side.

"What Sebastian does is none of your concern," Tabitha spat back. Her hands turned to fists and then relaxed again at her sides. Clenching, then relaxing. Clenching and relaxing.

Tabitha looked tired to Veronica. Veronica suspected part of the reason was because her clothing, the usual low rise jeans and tank top were layered in dirt and soot. Veronica supposed that she had fared pretty well considering she had walked away from an explosion. Sebastian looked in about the same condition as Tabitha, tired and dirty.

Quickly reading their minds Veronica came to realize neither one had fed yet. Not that it surprised her. Scarlet would be best advised to tread lightly with them at this moment. Of course, that's exactly what Veronica was hoping she *wouldn't* do. Despite being tired and hungry, Tabitha could still rip the new vampire to shreds in a matter of minutes if she so chose.

Am I alive, am I dead? Oh God where am I? Julie's words came shooting into Veronica's head. She turned her eyes to look at Julie. The human's eyes, Julie's eyes, were still closed but her heart rate was becoming a little stronger. She could smell the blood that had made its way down Julie's neck and hated herself for being drawn to it. She longed to lick it off.

Still applying pressure to Julie's neck, she distracted herself by shifting her attention back to the two vampires in the convenience store. One of the truckers, a short, stubby fellow, had heard a commotion and was making his way towards them. He made it halfway to them before he was stopped by Chyna, twirling yet another Jolly Pop in her mouth.

"Show me your truck, sweetie," she hooked her arm into his and turned him back the way he had come.

"Who are you, to tell me who I can or can't drink from?" Scarlet snarled, but she straightened up from her hunched position. Her fangs were still present, but her body seemed to release some of the tension. She reminded Veronica of a spoiled child. Defiant and testing her boundaries, but ultimately knowing her place.

"*I* lead this group. You come from *my* line. You answer to *me*, otherwise you won't live to see another day." Tabitha replied, her body also releasing some of the tension, her fists unclenching a final time as she folded her arms across her chest.

What to do about this one, Tabitha's thoughts came through to Veronica. *Perhaps Veronica was correct all along, we should have drained her and ditched the body with the car.*

You still can! Kill her and be done with it! Veronica would have loved for the power to implant her thoughts into other vamps' minds at that moment. Tabitha was so close to seeing things her way. So close. If only there was a way to push her over the edge.

Scarlet didn't reply but simply glared at Tabitha and Sebastian as she stormed past them and out of the store.

"Defy me again Scarlet and I'll drive a stake through your heart myself," Tabitha shouted after her. The group watched silently as she crossed the parking lot and over the I-95 before disappearing into the woods.

"So fucking tired of this bullshit!" Tabitha bellowed as she stepped back through the broken glass window. Noticing a large green recycle bin, situated just outside of the front door she gave it a hefty kick, sending it halfway across the parking lot and landing close to the gas pumps. The top fell open, spilling the contents onto the pavement. "Fuck!" she screeched.

Tabitha, followed by Sebastian walked over to Julie and Veronica. "Move out of the way," she commanded, giving Veronica's shoulder a shove. She looked up at Sebastian. "Go and feed; it won't be long before the sun rises."

Sebastian nodded, turned on his heel and sprinted off to find his lucky victim. The man in the electric blue Freightliner won the honour.

Dropping to one knee Tabitha bit into her wrist, blood began to seep from the wound. She moved to bring her wrist to Julie's mouth, but Veronica's hand closed over her wrist stopping her.

"She doesn't want to be turned," Veronica stated, keeping a firm grasp on Tabitha's wrist.

"First off, I'll turn her if I damned well please. Secondly, I have enough problems with the group of you running off half-cocked, to even consider adding a new member to our little family. Thirdly, unless she's already died with my blood in her, which she hasn't, she won't turn." A grin spread across Tabitha's face for the first time since she'd arrived there. "Let's just hope she doesn't have a motor vehicle accident or slip in the bathtub and break her neck when she gets home."

Tabitha jerked her wrist out of Veronica's grasp, placing it over Julie's mouth. Julie gagged and spit up the metallic tasting liquid, but some was still going down. Within minutes her face, which had turned a ghastly grey, began to return to its normal creamy beige. Ricardo who had been kneeling to the right of her, pulled her into his arms.

"I'm fine," Julie gasped, her eyes fluttering open.

Standing, Tabitha made her way to the trucks, jumped onto the side of a large double cab red Volvo, and tested the door. It was locked. She smashed it in with her fist, reached in and unlocked it. Opening the door she slipped in, not even bothering to close the door behind her.

"Julie, I'm..." Veronica started.

"No...no, stay away from me! You're just like the rest of them," Julie spat shaking her head as Ricardo helped her to her feet. Realizing the danger had passed, Sandy emerged from her hiding spot and walked slowly across the convenience store floor. Spotting Julie, who was leaning on Ricardo for support and covered in blood, she quickly made her way to the trio. She took up position on the other side of Julie, draping Julie's arm over her shoulders in much the same manner as Ricardo had done.

"I can explain," Veronica tried again. "It had to be like this."

"I almost died and *you* wanted it to happen. I risked *my own life* not so long ago to save you. Or have you already forgotten that?" Flames rose up in Julie's eyes as she raged at Veronica. Rage and resentment came to the surface, not only over what had happened tonight, but over the situation in general. Rage for the hell she and her two co-workers had been experiencing for the past several months, because of *them*, because of *her*!

"You don't understand," Veronica sighed, shaking her head. How could she blame Julie for the way she was feeling? She had every right to feel that way. She had been a virtual prisoner for months, they all had. They all had a right to be casting dirty, disgusted looks at her.

Ricardo looked up at the sky; Julie followed his gaze. The night was beginning to give way to daylight, the sun, threatening to show its face. "You had better go. We wouldn't want to see you and your crew burnt to a crisp out here."

Veronica was tempted to search their minds, search their thoughts, but was afraid of what she'd find there. Besides, she already had a good idea of what she'd find.

"Let's go," a male voice shouted from over by the parking area. Sebastian and Tabitha had finished their feeding and were about to head back to the farm.

Not bothering to take a look back at the three humans glaring at her, she joined the other vampires as they made their way back across the I-95 and into the woods.

Julie surveyed the broken window, then the dozens of empty beverage bottles scattered across the parking lot, then finally the semi-truck with the window broken out. She shook her head. She had no idea how she was going to explain this mess when the manager came into work. She looked down at her watch. They had less than an hour before the morning crew arrived.

As if reading her thoughts Sandy asked, "How do we explain this?"

"Hell if I know," she took the energy that she had remaining and pulled herself up so she was standing of her own accord. She was still a little wobbly, but was able to regain her balance.

Weebles wobble but they don't fall down, Chyna's words taunted in her head.

Shut up! Her mind shouted back.

"What I do know is that we're going to find a way to kill them. Kill them all," she vowed. She was done playing servant to them, done being scared. Come hell or high water she'd find a way to kill them all, once and for good. Even Veronica.

Julie's knees went weak a second time, but Ricardo caught her. "Come on, sit down in the restaurant while Sandy and I clean this mess up.

Julie nodded allowing him to escort her to a booth in the diner. Using her arms as a pillow she laid her head down on the table in front of her and closed her eyes.

Chapter 6

It was like talking to a brick wall when it came to discussing anything with Tabitha. Veronica peered out of the window. Two semi-trucks with full length trailers and occupants still remained in their back yard. She was curious to see how Tabitha planned on disposing those. She couldn't imagine Tabitha crashing the final set. Two sets of trucks coming to a fiery demise on the same stretch of interstate in the matter of a week was suspicious enough, but three sets was really pushing it. When she searched Tabitha's thoughts she came up blank. Tabitha had no solution as of yet.

"You realize she is only going to continue to cause trouble, and risk exposing us," Veronica cautioned as Tabitha entered the kitchen.

"It's none of your concern, Veronica," Tabitha stated flatly. Her gaze captured Veronica's and told her to back off the topic.

But she couldn't. She wouldn't.

"She went against your off-limits orders. She blatantly disobeyed," she protested.

"I said already it's none of your concern. I will deal with it."

"Like you're going to deal with those trucks out there," she nodded to the window, hooking a thumb in their direction.

"Some vampires when turned are harder to rein in than others. She will come around. And yes *I* will deal with it."

Veronica fell silent for a moment, listening for Tabitha's thoughts. She was still coming up blank. If going by Tabitha's actions and words, it looked as though she was no better off today in her quest to rid them of Scarlet than she was yesterday. She had no idea what the fascination with Scarlet was all about. It made no sense. She never figured Tabitha to be a believer in second and third chances.

"If you're through with the third degree and lecture, then I will ask your permission to retire to my quarters," her tone dripped sarcasm as Tabitha brushed past Veronica and headed for the staircase, which led to the upstairs bedrooms.

Veronica said nothing, but simply watched her go.

She could *feel* Scarlet's presence before she emerged from the living room. Scarlet preferred to sleep in the basement. Veronica felt that was ironically appropriate considering her feeling towards the newest vampire.

"Talking about me again were we?" Scarlet asked as she sauntered into the kitchen.

Veronica snorted. "You're not worth wasting my breath on."

"Ohhh, someone is a Miss Cranky Pants today. Perhaps if you got down from your high horse from time to time, you'd be more pleasing to be around."

"I think my attitude may have a lot to do with the company present."

Scarlet's head fell back as she laughed - a loud, hearty laugh. "Get use to it, I'm here to stay darlin'," she promised. Turning on her heel she exited the kitchen, heading back to her sanctuary in the basement.

"Hey Scarlet," Veronica called after her.

Scarlet stopped and made a half turn towards Veronica, raising an eyebrow at her. "Yah?"

"Next stake that heads toward your heart, will be at *my* hand. I promise *I* won't miss."

"We'll see darlin', we'll see."

She glared at the back of her nemesis as she sashayed away, her hips swaying in their usual provocative way under the sheer material of the red slip she had on, which fell to mid-thigh. *Everything about her stinks like whore and trouble*, Veronica fumed, clenching her fists at her sides.

She hadn't been able to sleep yet today. The previous night's events kept replaying themselves in her mind. Heaving a sigh, Veronica followed the path upstairs that Tabitha had previously taken. She'd need all her energy for the coming night; she had a feeling the humans were about to become a lot less hospitable from now on.

****

The vampires might now know that she kept a stake on her at all times, but Julie didn't care. They never did find the stake she had plunged into Scarlett's chest last night, so she had wrangled up a new one before coming to work. She stashed in its usual place hidden out of sight in the waistband of her faded blue jeans, against her back. If she had an opportunity she would use it; there was no doubt in her mind about that. She had missed once, but she wasn't about to miss a second time.

By the time the manager had come in that morning, Ricardo and Sandy had succeeding in cleaning up all the broken glass and collecting all the stray recyclables. The remainder of the night and morning had been yet another quiet one allowing for them to tidy up as much as possible, without the distraction of customers. *Thank God for small miracles*, Julie thought.

When the manager, a middle-aged man with a few extra pounds and more than his fair share of grey hair asked what had happened to the window they claimed it had been vandals; the same vandals that had broken out the side window of the trucker's cab.

The video footage had also been of no use, the disk had somehow gotten erased. Of course, the three night shift workers knew how it got erased, since they had done it themselves, but claimed ignorance on the subject.

Now back at work that night, she noticed he had wasted no time replacing the window. She was also relieved to see that it was extremely busy. Busy enough that it might keep them away for a night, though deep down she knew that wouldn't be the case. They would come; they always came. In busy periods like this one they simply waited a little longer before emerging from the woods and crossing the interstate.

As the sun dipped behind the horizon, and the sky began to darken, Julie kept her eyes on the tree line, waiting for them to appear. They failed to show at their usual time. Vehicles came and went, but there was no sign of the vampires. Ricardo and Sandy were also very busy tonight. The restaurant was still close to halfway full at eleven pm.

Between customers, Julie took a moment to stroll up to the newly replaced window and peer out in the direction of the parking area. All twenty slots were full of semi-trucks and trailers. Looking back into the store she noted there was no one in the convenience store section of the truck stop so she chanced stepping out into the cool fall night air.

Once outside she felt it. Felt *them*. She couldn't see them, but just knew they were there, just barely under the cover of the tree line. They were waiting for the truck stop to clear out, just as she had suspected. Tabitha was concerned that with so many people wandering about Scarlet would do something stupid and cause more trouble than she already had. Maybe even expose them, so Tabitha had ordered them all to wait.

Julie had no idea how she knew all that. Maybe it was a guess based on everything that had transpired since Scarlet had been taken in by them, but she didn't think so. She *knew*. She also knew that Tabitha was contemplating ending Scarlet's immortality and that she and Veronica were now in the 'outs'. She wasn't tapping into the vampires' *thoughts* exactly, but it was almost like she was tapping into their *emotions*.

"What have you done to me?" She whispered into the night air, filled with wonder. She felt a chill shimmy up her spine, one not provoked by the breeze, but by fear. What if she was turning? While she had been only semi-conscious she had been aware that it was Tabitha's blood that had brought her back from the brink of death. Tabitha had stated she couldn't turn unless she died, died with the vampire blood in her. What if she had, in fact, died? Maybe her heart had stopped for a brief moment, just long enough for the blood to work its magic?

She ran her tongue over her upper teeth. No traces of fangs. But fangs came out when vamps were in a heightened emotional state. Perhaps she just hadn't gotten to that point yet. She shook her head and dismissed the concept as paranoia. Newborn vampires couldn't walk in sunlight without experiencing pain. She had been out most of the day with no problems at all.

No, she wasn't a vampire, she was certain of that. But there was no denying something was different. She *felt* different. It was inexplicable, but true. Like at this very instant she *knew* Tabitha was deciding that the truck stop was finally slow enough that they could now cross the interstate and have their nightly meal.

Julie rushed into the truck stop and then into the adjoining restaurant in search of Sandy and Ricardo. Both were standing by the restaurant checkout. Two truck drivers paid their respective bills and sauntered past Julie, the first one ignored her completely while the second one stopped and gave her a once over, pausing at her breasts, before trailing after his buddy.

"They're here," Julie announced.

A look of anxiety flashed across Sandy's face and eyes, while anger grew in Ricardo's. He looked out of the large plate glass window which travelled the length of the restaurant. "Where? I don't see them."

"They're there, trust me. They'll be clearing the woods any moment," Julie confirmed. "Just a forewarning."

Both restaurant staff gave her puzzled looks, then nodded.

Julie hadn't even gotten back to her normal spot behind the cash register before she saw Tabitha break free from the tree line, quickly followed by the rest of her crew. This time however, there seemed to be a sombreness about the way they walked, about how they carried themselves, which struck Julie as unusual.

"See you next week, Julie," a husky male voice called from the truckers' lounge.

Looking over, Julie noticed Jimmy heading for the exit. Knowing he had her attention Jimmy gave her a broad smile, and waved.

Jimmy stopped there once a week, like clockwork. If it was Wednesday night then Jimmy would be there. Jimmy was a hell-of-a nice guy and had been used as food more than once over the past few months. She smiled and waved back, watching him leave and head in the direction of his truck parked in the lot.

As they crossed the interstate Tabitha's emotions seemed to become clearer to Julie. "Relax! Take a deep breath and relax," Julie muttered to herself. Isn't that what those mystics and psychics on television did in order to tell the future? *Yah, but that's make believe*, her reason argued back at her. *But it couldn't hurt though*, she told herself firmly, vetoing reason's feeble argument.

They were crossing the parking lot now, but to her surprise they didn't head straight for the store like they always did. The only one still on course for the store was Chyna. The others headed directly to the trucks. Chyna was the only one of the crew that seemed to be her normal self. She walked with her usual arrogance, the skirt of her zebra striped sundress whipping around her thighs as she walked. Julie had to hand it to her; Chyna could really pull off zebra print, not an easy task for most women.

"What are they doing?" Sandy poked her head into the convenience store area and asked in a voice barely louder than a whisper.

Julie knew exactly the underlying question behind Sandy's concern. Why isn't Sebastian coming in to torment me? Julie shrugged. "Dunno."

As Chyna reached the entrance, Sandy turned and scurried back into the restaurant.

So much for being my wingman, Julie mused wryly. As she craned her neck to see into the restaurant, she noticed it was still quite busy. Perhaps that's why Chyna was the only one making her way into the store.

Chyna entered the store and headed straight for the front counter, her eyes fixed on the Jolly Pop display.

Well that explains that mystery, Julie thought, leaning her elbows on the counter pretending to be more relaxed than she felt, *She needs her usual Jolly Pop fix for the night.*

Chyna lifted herself up on the counter, sitting in her usual spot next to the beef jerky display. She plucked a blue Jolly Pop from the sucker display and offered it to Julie. "Want one?" she asked cheerfully.

Expecting Julie to say no she began to pull the wrapper from the sucker.

On impulse Julie replied, "Yah. I would. Thanks." She reached her hand out for it.

Chyna furrowed her brow, giving her a look of confusion laced with annoyance. It was the last blueberry in the display. Julie had just messed with her normal routine. Julie was supposed to refuse. After a moment she shrugged and passed it over, looked back at the display and plucked out a yellow one. Banana flavour. She pulled off the wrapper and popped it into her mouth, passing the used wrapper to Julie. "The blueberry sucks anyhow," Chyna muttered to herself.

Julie fought to keep herself from sniggering. She succeeded, keeping her facial features blank.

"Why didn't the others come in?" Julie asked casually. She twirled the Jolly Pop in her mouth. She had to hand it to Chyna, the blueberry was pretty damned good, despite Chyna's claim that it sucked.

Chyna swung her legs back and forth for a moment before responding. "They're all pissed at each other. Veronica with Tabitha and Scarlet. Tabitha with Scarlet. Scarlet with all of us." She looked at Julie, her black eyes gleaming. "They are all being such stick-in-the-muds."

"So why are you here when the rest are feeding?" Julie pretended she couldn't care less about the answer, but was just trying to entertain Chyna and make small talk.

"Like I said, they're not being very fun to be around right now." She gave Julie a look that implied she must be stupid to have not reached that conclusion on her own.

Julie reached behind her, grasping the stake in her right hand.

Chyna laughed, "You can be really comical Julie."

Julie didn't answer just held the vampire's gaze.

"You can't kill me. I'd have your throat torn out by the time that stake was removed from your jeans. By the way, we are all aware of your intentions," she nodded towards the still busy restaurant. "And theirs."

Julie's eyes narrowed, but she relaxed her grip on the stake. She'd have to come up with an alternative plan. Or bide her time until the vampires relaxed around them again - relaxed enough to let their guards down.

"You didn't play nicely with Scarlet last night, Julie," she giggled, twirling the banana Jolly Pop in her mouth, "Scarlet won't soon forget about that, you know."

"Why do *you* care?" Julie asked suspiciously, her eyes narrowing at Chyna.

Chyna shrugged and laughed, "I don't. Your knowing won't change a thing." She pulled the depleted Jolly Pop from her mouth and examined the stick. She handed the stick to Julie to discard then grabbed another pop from the rack - strawberry this time. Sliding off the counter to her feet she began walking to the exit.

"You planning on paying for those?" Julie asked, knowing the answer, but for some reason couldn't resist asking the question.

"You're still alive, aren't you?" Chyna replied, not bothering to look back as she pushed the glass door open. As she exited a trucker whose looks reminded Julie of a California surfer, tan included, was just entering. She ran a finger across his lean t-shirt clad chest. "Hey good looking," she purred.

He stepped back, allowing her to pass by. She breezed past him, without another look in his direction. He stood, holding the door open with his boot clad foot watching her slender hips sway under her skirt as she headed for the semi-trucks to the left of the parking lot.

By 2 am the customers had all but cleared out of the restaurant. The store and truckers' lounge were also empty. Since Chyna's visit earlier that evening, Julie hadn't heard nor seen any of the vampires. She did, however, still *feel* their presence. By 4 am the feeling that they were close faded, leading her to believe that either they had gone home already or that perhaps the feelings she was getting from Tabitha were simply a figment of her imagination.

Not long before the new shift of workers started, enabling the trio of graveyard shift workers to go home, Ricardo and Sandy came over from the restaurant, confusion written all over their faces.

"Why didn't they come in?" Sandy asked hesitantly.

Julie smiled at her, shoving her hands in the back pockets of her jeans. "Perhaps I scared them off," she joked.

Sandy raised an eyebrow and gave her a look which said her joke was hardly funny or reasonable.

"Well, what did Chyna want?" Ricardo asked crossing his arms over his chest.

"What she always wants. Her Jolly Pop fix." Julie shrugged and laughed. She chose to keep her newly suspected 'ability' to herself for the time being. At least until she had a better idea of what it was, if, indeed, it was anything.

The three looked at each other, bewilderment written on each of their faces. All wondered the same thing: *what would tomorrow night bring*? The peace surely couldn't last forever.

****

But it did last; the peace and the silence. For over a week from the day of Julie's near-death experience, the vampires would come each night, but would avoid the store and restaurant. Only Chyna would actually come into the store. She'd come in, get her Jolly Pop, shoot the shit with Julie for a short while, get bored, then take off towards the parked trucks in search of her dinner.

Julie found that her ability to sense the vampires continued; as a matter of fact, it got stronger with each passing day. She was finding that she could now not only sense Tabitha's emotions, but the others as well; no thoughts - at least not yet - just emotions.

She also realized that she was indeed still human. She hadn't turned and she was beyond relief over that discovery. Her sensing their emotions brought her a better understanding of who they were and, better yet, why they behaved as they did. She felt their rage, their arrogance, their fear, and even their loneliness.

It still didn't alter the fact that she hated them. The hatred raged on; the desire to drive a stake through their cold hearts still lingered, intensified even. The past couple of days she was beginning to feel their hunger, like an addiction. It didn't excuse them, but she understood their drive now - which made killing them all the more important, especially for a vampire like Scarlet who lacked the willpower to kick even mortal addictions. Her bloodlust terrified Julie. Scarlet would do *anything* for blood.

With Scarlet in their midst she realized that Tabitha was forced to keep them away from the store, away from people other than their victims, the truckers. But the fact that they were having to forego their nightly round of shits-and-giggles at the expense of the midnight shift was grating on all the vampires' nerves. Julie could foresee the whole situation coming to a head and soon. She and the others just had to wait it out and avoid the debris when the situation erupted.

Chapter 7

A pearl white Peterbilt pulled up into the lot. It was a beauty, lighting up the truck stop in an almost magical way. Lights and chrome galore; a trucker's dream truck if ever Julie had seen one. It pulled into an empty slot within the truck parking and the driver shut it down. It responded with a hiss. The night went dark once more.

Several minutes later, two men jumped down from the cab and made their way towards the store. Julie's heart fluttered nervously, something about them was not quite right. If she were Spiderman, she'd have said her 'spidey senses' were tingling. When they came close enough for her to examine them, she noticed they both had the same short, blond hair and the same ice-blue eyes. One looked several years older than the other, but it was clear they were related. Her best guess would be that they were brothers.

The younger one seemed to ignore Julie when he entered and made his way towards the restrooms, but the older one gave her a nod and smiled. The smile and intensity of the look in his eyes shot a thrilling jolt right through her. It reminded her of the feeling she would get when she was back in high school and the boy she had a crush on showed a hint of interest in her for the first time. She laughed at herself when she identified the feeling he was provoking within her. He made her feel giddy.

When he smiled, dimples appeared out of nowhere and stole at least five years from his age. She was guessing the youngest to be in his early thirties, leaving the older brother ranging somewhere in his middle thirties.

Julie returned the smile, watching as the older brother went into the truckers' lounge and headed for the telephones. Turning his back to her, he went about placing his call.

She had been so engrossed in the two brothers that she hadn't noticed Tabitha and her crew until they were already across the I-95 and making their way across the parking lot. She looked over towards the truckers' lounge and noticed the younger of the two had finished in the restroom and the two of them were now sitting at one of the tables talking.

The same panic that she had felt with Veronica seemed to overwhelm her with this pair as well. Leaving her counter she took a nervous look out of the window and decided she just might have enough time to warn them to get out. They appeared to be planning to spend the night bunked up at the truck stop. She wasn't quite sure how she was going to convince them to keep moving. She decided she would have to play it by ear.

They both looked up, as she jogged over to the table, giving her curious looks.

"You have to leave," she stated matter-of-factly. Without consideration for what she was doing Julie reached out and took hold of the older brother's hand, giving it a tug, urging him to get up.

"You're closing?" Smiling, he tilted his head and arched an eyebrow at her.

His smile was infectious. She found herself feeling foolish, but returned the smile anyhow. She took hold of the other man's hand as well, tugging at them both. "No. But you both have to leave. Now!"

The two shared a look, but neither would budge from their seats.

She heard the door swing open.

"Sannnndddyyy!" Sebastian's voice echoed throughout the store, lounge and restaurant.

Great, it's been two weeks since they've come in here and they pick tonight to do it, she growled to herself. Emotions began to flood through her, coming from both the group of vampires at the front of the store and the two men she was still grasping the hands of.

Both men jerked their heads around to see who had entered. Julie watched the older one's face darken, his smile fading. She and the two truckers watched as the remaining vampires entered the store. She felt anger coming from the two seated men.

This doesn't make sense, Julie thought. *I can't sense the emotions of humans.* She dropped their hands, which she now realized felt cool in her own and took a step back from them. Julie's mouth dropped open and she quickly covered it with her hand.

Her head spun back to the five vampires standing at the store entrance. Hatred and a hint of fear emulated from them. Their eyes were glued to the two men seated in front of her.

"Let's go," she heard the older one say to the younger one, as he stood. The younger brother nodded and followed suit.

As they stood, Julie was positive that they suddenly appeared larger than they previously were. Perhaps it was the way they stood tall, shoulders back, a deadly calm in their ice-blue eyes.

"The Queen's bitches!" Sebastian snarled. Julie focused her attention back to Sebastian. His fangs were bared and his eyes had turned blood red. Searching the faces of the four female vamps, she noticed they had also dropped their fangs in place, eyes turning red as well.

Queen's bitches? She looked back at the two men at her side. What did he mean by Queen's bitches? She wanted to ask, but remained silent.

****

Before coming to the truck stop tonight, Tabitha informed them that they would be going about their usual routine. She was sick of hiding in the woods, feeding and going back to the farmhouse. It was time Scarlet took responsibility for her own urges. The next slip up, the next time Scarlet endangered the group would be her last day as an immortal.

As Tabitha spoke Veronica had read her mind. She was deadly serious in her conviction. Scarlet on the other hand was seething, and still defiant. While her head had nodded in agreement with Tabitha's decision, she was nowhere close to bowing to Tabitha's will. It was only a matter of time before she would be rid of Scarlet for good, she was certain of that now.

As they approached the truck stop, Veronica's head began to become littered with thoughts. Most of them were the truckers' thoughts. Some missed their wives, girlfriends, kids. One was hoping a lot lizard would slither her way around the lot tonight. *Last place you'll find one of those mister*, Veronica thought. Others worried they may not get their loads to their destinations on time.

She heard the thoughts of Julie and the others, but two people at the station were different. She couldn't put her finger on it, but they weren't concerned about loads, or wives or anything of that sort. They were thinking about the arrival of the Queen - the arrival of *their* Queen. As the band of vampires grew closer to the convenience store entrance she came to have the feeling that she should know this Queen they were referring to. *The Queen was coming home.* The Queen?

It came to her... It was *her* Queen. *Their* Queen. Tabitha had never mentioned anything about the Vampire Queen. Come to think of it, she didn't recall Tabitha or Sebastian ever speaking of their kind's history or origins at all really.

As they entered the store Sebastian called out to Sandy as he usually did. He hadn't so much as gotten her name from his lips when he spun around, his fangs dropped, eyes red.

Veronica turned to see who he, and now the rest of the group were staring at. Julie was standing next to two good looking, blond haired men who were sitting at a table in the truckers' lounge. Without even realizing what was happening her own fangs dropped too and she assumed her eyes had turned as well, like a natural instinct when in the presence of these men.

Thoughts came flooding into her, like automatic gunfire:

Tabitha: *They're powerful. Old.*

Sebastian: *Fucking Queen's Vampires.*

The younger vampire: *Damn it, it's like the country is plagued with these ingrate vampires.*

The older vampire: *Five of them. Shouldn't be a problem to fight though.*

Younger vampire: *The dark skinned one is the leader. Fairly old.*

Older vampire: *Get out of my head vampire*! This was a command.

How did he? That was her own thought.

I also have the power to read minds, the older vampire informed her silently.

She blocked out the thoughts of the others, focusing solely on the older vampire. *Then you know I'm not one of them, not really. I want them dead as much as I suspect you two do*, she replied mentally.

His thoughts went blank momentarily before he resumed: *That's not our problem. We're not here to exterminate your group. A simple case of wrong place, wrong time. I warn you now, try and stop us from leaving and we'll kill you all.*

They've been keeping the humans working here hostage. The one to my left, she nodded towards Scarlet, *has nearly caused our kind to be exposed on numerous occasions.*

His mind went blank to her for another moment, then: *Not our concern. We have more pressing issues.* His mind blanked out to her a final time.

The two men stood and began to walk towards the exit. Their steel blue eyes never leaving Sebastian's for a moment.

"Pussy assed, motherfuckers," Sebastian spat after them as they strolled past.

"Sebastian," Tabitha spoke up, touching his arm, attempting to quiet him.

"Just like their bitch of a Queen. They're too spineless to stand up and fight. Run away ladies," he taunted, laughing as he spoke.

It was so fast that Veronica didn't see him coming. The older vampire came barrelling past her, knocking her to the floor with such a force that she was sent across the newly waxed floor, slamming her back into a wire potato chip rack.

Veronica shook her head and blinked. The oldest vampire had slammed Sebastian against the counter, holding him down with his large hand, by the neck; Sebastian's face planted flat against the countertop.

"Time to party!" Chyna squealed with excitement as she leapt onto the back of the vampire who was currently pinning Sebastian down.

The younger of the two Queen's vampires made a reach for Chyna, but was steamrolled by Tabitha. She hit him with an extraordinary amount of force, in a tackle that would have secured her a spot on a team in the NFL, and sent him sprawling through the new front window. Looking around, Veronica noticed the three humans were simply standing on the sidelines watching the action with their mouths open in shock.

Still clinging to the back of the older Queen's vampire, Chyna bit into his neck. Chyna seemed to get his attention enough that he loosened his hold on Sebastian to wrestle her off him and send her sailing from the store and into the truckers' lounge. His loosened hold was enough to allow Sebastian to break free. His fist smashed into the underside of the older Queen's vampire's jaw causing him to take a few steps backwards.

Scared for the humans, Veronica raced around the fighting vampires to Julie. "Come on," she commanded and felt relieved when Julie nodded. Looking at the store she realized the fight was now in full swing. Sebastian and Chyna were wrestling with the older Queen's vampire, while Tabitha and Scarlet seemed to have the upper hand with the younger one.

The vampires were too engrossed in the fighting to notice as she guided Julie into the restaurant, ushering the three nightshift workers into the back kitchen.

Once out back, Julie looked at Veronica with urgency, "they're going to kill each other!" She exclaimed, wide eyed.

"Let's hope so," Veronica agreed.

They could hear the crashing, glass breaking, screams and an assortment of snarls and groans coming from the store.

With the intensity of the fighting and the speed at which the thoughts were running through the vampires' heads, Veronica couldn't get a proper read on any of them. She only knew that so far, they were all alive.

"Julie?" Sandy said.

"Hmm," she turned to face Sandy.

"If we live through this, how are we going to explain the damage?"

Veronica grinned, "Tornado?"

They all laughed, although it was more a laugh of discomfort than of actual humour.

They were unsure exactly how long they hid out in the kitchen, but finally the commotion quietened, to the extent where you could literally hear a pin drop.

"Are they all dead?" Sandy asked hesitantly.

Veronica put a finger to her lips and shook her head. She motioned for them to stay in the kitchen so she could investigate. They readily agreed, nodding their heads in unison. As she left the kitchen and entered the restaurant she stepped lightly, though in truth it was a wasted effort, they'd be able to tell she was coming either way.

As she rounded the corner, she gasped. The convenience store looked like it had indeed been run through by a tornado. A number of the refreshment cooler glass panes were broken out. The new front window pane was now shattered and lying on the floor in fragments. There were food products sprawled across the floor, some still in their packaging, some open and plastered against the white ceramic tiles.

All of the vampires were alive. The two Queen's vampire's sat bloodied and exhausted near the truckers' lounge. The older of the two had a large gaping hole in his neck, blood still flowing from the wound. She glanced over to her right to see the rest of her own crew. If she thought the Queens vampires looked bad, then her family were near death. They all sat panting, bloodied, their clothing and hair out of place. Sebastian had a stake driven through his left shoulder. Close. But as the old saying goes: *close only applies to horseshoes and hand grenades.*

The two Queen's vampires, struggled to their feet. The left arm of the younger one seemed to hang loosely under his t-shirt sleeve.

"Damn it!" He cursed, looking over at his brother. "Give me a hand with this will you, Jacob?" He nodded his head towards his dislocated arm.

"Sure," the older vampire, identified as Jacob, replied. Standing on the left side of his brother, he grasped his shoulder with one hand and his upper arm with the other. "Ready?"

The younger vampire nodded, "Yah."

A sound that Veronica could only describe as a crunch came from the younger vampire's shoulder. He winced, but just for a split second. He moved his head from side to side and tested his arm, rolling it forwards then backwards.

Having reached the conclusion that his brother was fine, Jacob began walking towards the truck stop exit, his brother close on his heels. As he drew nearer, Veronica could actually see the gashes in his face and arms begin to heal themselves. The large gaping hole where Chyna had bitten a massive piece out of his neck looked grotesque, blood still flowing from it, though the flow was now no more than a faint trickle. She could almost *see* it healing before her very eyes. The regeneration of Tabitha and the others was good, very good in fact, but nothing like that of the two vampires coming towards her. She also noticed one additional difference; their eyes had turned from steel blue to pure white. She found herself wondering why.

Because we're born of the blood of our Queen, came the silent response from Jacob's mind to hers. *You've been bred from the King's blood*, his eyes sought out Tabitha, *Your sire has not fulfilled her obligation as your clan's leader to tell you about the bloodlines.*

Veronica didn't feel it was necessary to advise them it was actually Sebastian that had sired her and Scarlet. She simply nodded.

"This isn't over," Sebastian snarled, now attempting to pull out the stake, which appeared to be the thick trim off one of the store shelves.

Both of the Queen's vampires stopped in mid-stride, they were almost at the exit before they turned back to survey their four combat-worn foes.

"Pray for your sake that it *is*, vampire. Next time we won't be as kind as to spare your ungrateful and disrespectful lives." Jacob responded.

His brother nodded his agreement, adding: "Think twice next time you feel the need to speak ill of our Queen." Without another word they exited, heading off in the direction of their truck.

She could hear the trio of night workers slowly making their way into the restaurant, from the kitchen behind her.

Through a series of moans and grunts, Tabitha and the others slowly attempted to rise to their feet. As they stood, a couple of dark haired young women, dressed in cyber goth attire made their way towards the entrance of the convenience store. The taller of the two reached out for the door handle to enter and then stopped dead in her tracks, her friend stopping with her. They examined the condition of the store in disbelief, their eyes finally falling on the four badly bloodied and beaten vampires.

Without a word both young women started to slowly back up, keeping their shock and fear-filled eyes glued to the vampires. Once they reached what they felt was a safe distance from the vampires they turned and made a run for their car. They hopped in and sped off, the tires of the tiny vehicle squealing and leaving skid marks as they made their getaway.

Scarlet broke the silence in the store, "where the fuck, were you when we were having our asses handed to us?" She demanded, her eyes narrowing at Veronica.

Veronica pulled herself up to her full height of five foot two. "Protecting the humans," she replied, daring Scarlet to make something of it.

Scarlet made a hissing sound between her teeth, giving Veronica a disgusted look.

Chyna began laughing as she adjusted the ripped bodice of her dress. "Shit, what a mess in here," she eyed the trio of humans standing behind Veronica, "have fun with that."

"I'd like to enjoy a good laugh with you, but I have a stake in my goddamned shoulder, you assholes," Sebastian growled, still struggling to pull it out. As he stood, Veronica noticed that it had pierced straight through his body, the sharp bloody end sticking out of his back.

Scarlet approached him, pressed her body against the length of his and licked the side of his bloodied neck. "Their blood is delicious," she commented.

With his good arm, Sebastian pushed her away from him. "Either help or get the fuck away from me," he snarled, which caused Chyna to begin her high pitched hysterical laughter once more. A peculiar look came over Scarlet, before she also burst out laughing.

"Bunch of mindless idiots. I'll get it. Hold still," Tabitha commanded as she braced one hand on his chest. The other grasped the makeshift stake, "this is going to hurt like a bitch," she warned giving it a violent yank and pulling it free from his body.

Sebastian howled in agony, dropping back down to his knees, clutching at his shoulder.

"Don't be such a big baby Sebastian," Scarlet scolded. "I had a stake driven into my chest a week or so ago and didn't whine nearly as much as you." She turned and shot a venomous look in Julie's direction. Her look said that the matter was far from having been settled.

"What were the other vampires talking about? Who is the Queen? Why are their eyes white? How did Sebastian know they were the Queen's vampires?" Her questions were directed at Tabitha, being thrown out at her like automatic gunfire.

"We'll discuss it later," came the curt reply.

"When you get older you'll be able to smell the difference between us and them," Sebastian replied, rubbing his injured shoulder.

"Well, why..." Veronica was cut off in mid-sentence as Tabitha strode over to her, grasped her neck tightly and pinned her against the wall. Her feet dangled a foot off the floor. Veronica wriggled and gagged, trying to free herself from Tabitha's grip, but to no avail. Despite having, as Scarlet put it, her ass handed to her, Tabitha was still far more powerful than Veronica could dream of being. She stopped struggling.

"I said we'll discuss it later," Tabitha stated once more through clenched teeth, her fangs bared.

Veronica didn't say anything, simply nodded her agreement.

Tabitha released Veronica and her body slumped to the floor momentarily. She brought her left hand to her neck and felt blood. Tabitha's nails had pierced her skin. With a sigh, she pulled herself back up to her feet.

"Let's go feed," Tabitha ordered heading towards the broken pane glass window and stepping through it before adding, "The humans have a full night of cleaning ahead of them."

The vampires sniggered as they followed Tabitha out of the store, none bothering with the door, all simply stepping through the glass window. Veronica trailed behind reluctantly. She turned to look back at the mess and her heart went out to Julie and the others. They'd need a small miracle to get this place looking presentable. Not to mention there was no way they could replace all the broken glass, coolers, and products, which lay strewn across the floor.

"Sorry everyone, I truly am," she said, not daring to look them in the eye. Turning, she stepped out of the window and followed the others to the truck parking to find the lucky trucker she would feast on for the night.

Chapter 8

Julie walked through the store hesitantly, with a look of shock and horror in her eyes. She had no idea how they were going to fix the store. It wasn't possible. Wasn't humanly possible. They could get it cleaned, but there was no way the glass could be replaced on the cooler doors. The same went for the large glass front window pane which once again lay shattered on the floor.

Ricardo followed her around the store, also surveying the damage. "We'll never be able to cover this up Julie," he said placing a hand on her shoulder when she stopped behind the cash register. "Maybe we should call the police and tell them the truth."

"Are you insane!" Julie exclaimed looking up into his concerned face. "They'd kill us and you know it, track us down like dogs and kill us. Or worse."

She looked over at Sandy who was slumped against the wall separating the restaurant from the store, weeping softly, her face in her hands.

Ricardo lifted his hands in surrender, defeat in his eyes. "Then you need to tell us what were going to do before someone comes along."

They couldn't go to the police. But there was no way they could fix the place themselves. Clean it yes. Fix it no. She looked at the clock which flashed 2 am in bright red numbers. They still had plenty of time to execute a plan before management arrived in the morning.

Sandy sniffed a few times then looked up at her co-workers. "Maybe we'll get fired," she suggested with a hopeful tone to her voice.

Julie shook her head. "It wouldn't make any different. If we were fired, we'd still be compelled to come her at our normal time. If we were fired, the vampires would no longer have a use for us and would drain us dry and leave our corpses in a ditch somewhere."

"Oh my god," Sandy whispered, eyes wide with horror. She burst into a fresh bout of tears. Her long blond hair fell over her face as she dropped her face back into her hands, weeping.

"We were vandalized and robbed," Julie finally said.

"What?" Grasping her shoulders, Ricardo spun Julie around to face him. "Are you serious?"

Julie shrugged. "Sure. Why not," she motioned to the mess surrounding them, "Can you come up with a better explanation for all this?"

"But the security recordings?" he stammered

"We destroy everything in the office," Julie explained as she pulled open the stationery drawer under the cash register, and began searching for something. A minute later she produced a key, attached to a big red keychain in the shape of a transport truck. "Take this key and go into the office. Destroy everything in there."

"What?" Ricardo's mouth dropped open, shaking his head not quite believing what he was hearing. "What? No. What?"

Bending down, Julie opened a cabinet door under the countertop. She rummaged inside then pulled out a crowbar. She thrust the crowbar at him. "Here. Make sure you destroy all the recording equipment and all stored CDs. Make it look legit."

Ricardo accepted the crowbar. "Look Julie. I don't think you're thinking clearly." His dark brown eyes caught hers. "We could go to jail for this."

Julie laughed. Her laugh was hollow and shrill. A laugh that she would expect to hear coming from Scarlet or Chyna. "Going to jail is the least of our worries." *Might even be the best thing that could happen to us, considering the circumstances*, she thought but kept that to herself.

"Fine. I'll do it myself then. Just start cleaning out here." She made a motion to grab the crowbar, but he jerked it out of her reach. He held it high enough that even as she made a jump for it, her fingertips couldn't quite make contact with it.

"No. I'll do it," he finally said. "When I'm done and you're sure the vamps have left for the night we'll call the police and do as you said, pretend it was a robbery and they trashed the place for kicks." He looked over at Sandy who had finally gotten control of herself and was now sitting on the floor, hugging her knees to her chest, listening intently. "Is the plan fine with you?"

Sandy nodded

Ricardo looked at Julie, who had stopped reaching for the crowbar and stood in front of him, arms crossed. "Alright."

"Alright," Ricardo nodded, satisfied. Taking a deep breath he marched off in the direction of the manager's office.

As he walked off, Julie turned to look out into the parking lot. It was quiet, peaceful. Looking further out she noticed the five vampires disappearing into the woods. She then realized this was the first time since the battle had begun that she was able to sense their emotions. What she felt coming from them brought her blood to a boil. As she, Ricardo and Sandy were left yet again, trying to cover up their mess, they headed home feeling content, happy and at ease.

****

Jacob's younger brother, Devlon started to chuckle in the passenger seat of the massive pearl Peterbilt. They had left the truck stop roughly an hour earlier and were a solid seventy miles north of there. Devlon had kept silent for the duration of the drive so far but he couldn't help but bring it up now. Jacob could have read his thoughts, but they had an agreement, no mind reading amongst family so, to Devlon's knowledge, Jacob never did.

Jacob took his eyes off the highway for a brief moment to shoot Devlon an annoyed glare. "Dare I ask what you are finding so amusing?"

Devlon sobered up a bit, trying to wipe the grin from his face but failing. "That little wildcat sure took a chunk out of your neck there." He leaned in closer to the large, gaping hole which still remained in his brother's neck. "I think I can see the bone. It's fuckin' disgusting."

"Yah, thanks," Jacob could feel the wound healing itself as he drove. It didn't seem to be healing quite as quickly as he would have liked.

"It felt good though didn't it?" Devlon prompted.

With a sigh, Jacob shifted his eyes off the road again to glare at his younger brother once more. "The she-devil tore a huge chunk of my neck out with her teeth. Good isn't exactly how I would describe the feeling." In fact, it was one of the most painful injuries he had endured in over two centuries. He kept that information to himself. If vampires could catch diseases he was quite certain he would have needed to see a doctor to get a rabies shot or something of the sort.

"Huh?" Devlon looked momentarily confused then waved his hand in the air. He was way beyond the neck topic. "I mean the fight. It felt good. It's been a long time since we've kicked some King's vampires' ass." He shadow boxed in his seat, giving the air a one-two punch, before settling back down in the seat.

Jacob laughed. "They weren't much competition. Hell two of them were newborns, and one barely a few years old."

Devlon began to laugh again.

"What now?"

Wasn't it one of the young ones that gave you that nice little war wound?" He pointed to Jacob's mangled neck.

"You're an asshole."

"What about the fifth vampire - the one with the short black and red hair? She didn't jump in. What was her deal?"

Jacob reached up into the visor and snatched up a pair of black designer sunglasses and put them on. The sun was beginning to rise. He and his brother were too old to be killed by the sun anymore, but driving in the daytime without the glasses would give him a smashing headache.

"She can read minds," Jacob replied.

"Read minds? Wow. Not too often you come across one of the King's bloodline with *that* ability."

Jacob shrugged. "It happens. We've come across a few over the years." Seeing his exit he hit the turn signal, checked his mirrors, was satisfied it was safe to change lanes and pulled the truck, hauling over forty thousand pounds of freight, off onto the exit ramp.

"So what did she want?" Devlon was insistent.

Jacob heaved a loud sigh before answering, "She wanted us to kill the others."

"That's weird." Devlon sat back in the beige leather seat thinking over the information, "Did she say why?" he finally asked.

"Said something about the humans being held hostage. They were risking exposing our kind. Bullshit like that. I told her it wasn't our concern." Jacob slowed the truck down, as he manoeuvred a tight turn in the off-ramp.

Devlon sat up straight in his seat. "Maybe it should be."

The GPS informed them, it its chipper female voice, that they were now two miles away from their destination.

"We have more pressing concerns right now, brother." Jacob informed him, exiting the ramp and merging onto the highway.

Devlon was about to protest, but could tell his brother's mind was made up. Maybe he was right. The vampires weren't the Sinclair brothers' top priority at the moment. He still couldn't shake the feeling that they should go back. *Needed* to go back. The thing about Devlon Sinclair's hunches was that they rarely, if ever, failed him.

****

"What were they talking about Tabitha?" Veronica asked yet again. Tabitha had gathered the "family" into the living room for a meeting. She claimed she was going to tell the three newer vampires, Chyna, Veronica and Scarlet everything they needed to know about their bloodlines. This was the information Veronica had been waiting to hear since she'd been reborn.

Tabitha sighed, as she leaned back against the oversized brown plush armchair. She draped one shapely jean clad leg over the arm, letting it sway back and forth as she made herself comfortable.

She didn't need to begin speaking for Veronica to start getting an idea of why she had never spoken about the other vampires and their bloodlines. Veronica was realizing now that Tabitha liked the idea of the younger vampires believing she was all-powerful, all knowing, and one of the best ways to keep the others believing that was to keep them ignorant.

It was beginning to occur to her that Tabitha was just as much a young vampire as the rest of the family was in comparison to others who walked the earth. She couldn't blame Tabitha from keeping that information to herself; knowledge is power and Tabitha loved having all the power. With the exception of her questionable decision to turn Scarlet, Veronica admired the fact that she was as smart as she was ruthless.

"From what we know, our species were born from two vampires. The King and Queen," Tabitha began.

Veronica settled herself between Chyna and Scarlet on the large sofa which matched the armchair in which Tabitha was sitting. She noted with amusement that despite their indifferent attitude towards learning about their kind, they both seemed to be on edge, waiting to hear everything.

"Not even the King and Queen remember their exact age, I won't get into the mythological origins shit, but they'd both pretty fuckin' old. Ancient. And powerful that's all you need to know about that," She waved her hand in the air as if dismissing the rest of that part of the story. "Vampires are split into two clans, the King’s and the Queen’s. We are from the King's as you may have already guessed. The vamps we fought were from the Queen's bloodline."

"Fucking Queen's vampires," Sebastian cut in, rubbing his bare shoulder in a subconscious gesture as it was now almost completely healed.

"The main difference between the two bloodlines is that our eyes turn red, while theirs turn white," Tabitha explained.

"And their smell," Sebastian added, "Once you have enough contact with them you'll be able to smell them before you see them."

Smell? Didn't smell any different to me. Veronica turned her attention to Sebastian, sitting on the arm rest of Tabitha's chair, bare-chested and with a pair of worn blue jeans on. "So what of their Queen?"

"She pissed off a couple of centuries ago," he smirked at her then continued, "just as well; she was all about discipline and keeping our existence secret. Rules. Order. Blah, blah, blah."

"But there are rumours that she is returning. The King isn't pleased," Tabitha added.

"Why?" Chyna asked, speaking for the first time since they had gathered in the living room that afternoon.

"Pfft. Who knows?" Sebastian scoffed.

"Better yet, who cares?" Tabitha agreed with a laugh. "It's all a bunch of political nonsense." She looked at Sebastian and gave him a wink, "We play by our own rules right, baby?"

Sebastian gave her a wink in return, "that's right baby."

Veronica chanced a look at Scarlet. She seemed to be soaking up every ounce of information they were giving like a sponge. It was a little disconcerting to her. Veronica could tell where her mind was heading. She wanted to find the King. Veronica almost burst out laughing when she pried deeper into Scarlet's thoughts to reveal Scarlet was already attempting to form plots to align herself with the King. *Gold digger of the vampire world,* Veronica thought with a silent chuckle.

Tabitha stood, finished with her brief history lesson for the day. She began to walk past the sofa where the youngest vampires still sat, all three mulling over the new information in their heads. "Just don't get any ideas about running with vampires from the Queen's Clan, they're few in numbers and our kinds mix like water and oil."

"But water and oil don't mix," Scarlet interjected.

Veronica couldn't restrain herself from rolling her eyes. *If it hadn't been Scarlet who made that observation, it would have been Chyna,* she thought.

"Exactly my point," Tabitha replied. She continued out of the living room and towards the stairs to the bedrooms. She stopped at the foot of the stairs before turning back towards them. "There are rumours of a war forming. That's why we need to move out of here soon. We need to keep on the road. Keep under the radar until the dust settles."

If all the King's vampires were like Chyna and Scarlet, Veronica feared there wouldn't be many left once, as Tabitha put it, the dust settled.

****

Jacob looked over at his brother, who currently had his seat reclined and was sleeping soundly with a sheet covering his body. Devlon still hadn't gained enough resistance to the sun to be able to drive during the day. Jacob was able to power through it. Just like no human was alike, no vampire is born alike either. Their resistance to sun, their abilities, their strengths, and so forth were all a result of who they were as a human and who it was that had sired them. And in particular, which bloodline they came from.

Jacob was sired from the Queen herself, given the purest of all blood to be reborn, a number of centuries ago. Several years after he was turned, he turned his brother Devlon. They had both received some of the more desirable of abilities, Jacob could read minds, whereas, Devlon could dream-walk and had premonitions from his dreams. Other than the Queen, Devlon was the only vampire that Jacob was aware of that could get premonitions.

His train of thought led him to start thinking of Veronica. Reading minds was also one of the rarer talents a vampire could possess; it was almost unheard of in the King's spawns. What made her so special that she would happen to be granted that power? He rapped his fingers on the steering wheel, in time with a Van Halen song on the radio, as the truck continued to sail along towards their destination.

Jacob and Devlon were now on the interstate headed south again for New York City. They were to go to a club called Club Vampire, which was run by two of the most notorious of the Queen's vampires Nigel and Marcus. The Queen was due to arrive there sometime next week. She was resurfacing to reclaim the throne after secluding herself from the vamps for over two hundred years.

It was about time.

The King had been working hard at building a small army of his own vampires while she was away. As they say, while the cat's away the mice will play. This was bad, very bad. A good example would be the group of vampires they had encountered at the truck stop just a day ago. There was a reason why the Queen required selective "breeding" as she called it, or to be more accurate: selective "turning." Apparently, the King and his clan of miscreants had failed to get that memo.

"Go back!" Devlon screamed as he bolted upright in his seat. Startled, Jacob swerved the truck. It jumped onto the wrong lane barrelling towards oncoming traffic. The trailer pulled to the side, threatening to tip the entire rig. Jacob swerved once more, pulling the truck back into the correct lane, just barely missing an oncoming silver half ton. He felt a jarring at the back end, then a squealing of tires. *Guess I didn't quite miss them after all,* he mused.

With a couple more near collisions avoided, Jacob finally had the truck under control and cruising down the highway. He ran a shaky hand through his blond hair, flipped off the radio then turned to glance at his brother. "What the fuck Devlon! I almost flipped the truck!"

Devlon's eyes were pure white as he looked around frantically, still only half-conscious. "We need to go back!" He screamed a second time, locking his eyes onto Jacob.

Jacob shook his head, "Sorry brother, we have places to be. The humans can fend for themselves."

"It's the Queen!" A look of horror appeared on Devlon's face as he clutched at Jacob's shoulder; then fell back against the seat thrashing about. His eyes were still open, fangs bared.

"What the hell?" Jacob muttered under his breath.

Jacob looked over at him once more. It was apparent Devlon was still in the premonition. From the look on his face it was bad. Really bad. Seeing a rest area coming up he signalled and pulled off the highway.

"Scarlet. No!" Devlon bellowed, his head whipping from side to side.

"Wake up! Devlon, wake up!" Jacob leaned over his brother, taking hold of his shoulders and shaking him hard.

Devlon's body stopped thrashing, his head became still and his eyes closed. His breathing seemed to go back to normal, steady breaths.

Jacob waited. Five minutes. Ten minutes. Fifteen minutes went by before he finally saw his brother stirring. Hesitantly, Devlon opened his eyes. They were now back to the steel blue colour they normally were.

Jacob let out a sigh of relief as he sunk back into his seat. He let his head fall back against the headrest. "You gave me a scare," he chuckled as he turned his head so his eyes could meet Devlon's.

"We need to go back. Back to the vampires at the truck stop," Devlon said slowly, his voice barely more than a whisper.

"We have responsibilities. We have..." His voice trailed off as he watched Devlon shake his head, with conviction.

"We have to go back. It's Scarlet."

"The skanky vampire from the truck stop? The one wearing the corset?" Jacob questioned, his brow furrowing, then added, "She's a newborn. She's unimportant."

Devlon smiled a grim smile and shook his head. "If we don't kill her and the rest of the group, she's going to kill our Queen."

Chapter 9

If there was a hell Julie was convinced, as she stood in the middle of the convenience store, that she was living it right now. That morning she, Sandy and Ricardo hadn't been able to leave the truck stop until close to 1 pm. They had followed through with their plan, and got their stories coordinated as they destroyed evidence and told potential customers they were closed for renovations. No one questioned them, but most gave them curious looks as they walked back to their vehicles. Once everything - right down to hiding the money from the store and restaurant resister so it would appear to be a robbery was done - and they felt it looked legitimate, they called the police and their manager.

The police arrived shortly before their manager. The three of them and the truckers in the semi-trucks parked in the lot were questioned and the place was searched for possible evidence. They came up with nothing, but seemed suspicious. Perhaps Julie was simply being paranoid, but she didn't think so. The detective who was heading the investigation was a middle aged man, clean shaven, wearing horn-rimmed glasses. He seemed to have a keen sense for bullshit and considering the amount they were shovelling to him, she was shocked they hadn't been arrested on the spot.

Their story was simple. The place was vacant of customers at the time, which it had been, that part was the truth. A dark van, of which they couldn't tell the make, drove up to the store. Five men jumped out wearing ski masks and filed into the convenience store waving guns. One robbed her in the store, while another went into the restaurant. As the first two were grabbing the money the others were busy defiling the store. They told the detective and later their boss that they had no clue why they destroyed the store in the process, but guessed by the amount of pleasure they seemed to be getting from it, that they must have just done it for a laugh.

They were asked questions like, could it have been the same people as the previous incident? They responded they didn't know. Were they driving the same vehicle? They responded they didn't know. How much money did they get? And did they think that was their main objective, to rob the place? They said they didn't know.

Once done being questioned, the detective made the comment that there seemed to be a whole lot that they didn't know. An unusual amount considering there were three people there as witnesses. Again, they shrugged and claimed they had no comment.

Their boss was also a little curious when they told him they would all be more than happy to work their normal shifts as usual that night. Little did he know that they'd be there regardless of whether they were employed by the company or not. The vampires made sure of that.

So they came. And they waited. Angry, terrified, confused. A slew of emotions were flowing between them as they waited for the sun to fall far enough over the horizon for the vamps to arrive. Since the majority of the store was destroyed Julie was told to assist in the restaurant which had been untouched by the vandals. Yet another thing that made the detective curious.

Why had they left the restaurant untouched? They told the detective they didn't know.

Once she and her co-workers had finally been released to go home, they prepared for tonight. Prepared for what might be their final day with the vampires. Julie instructed them to bring in anything they had that could be used as a stake. She went to visit the local vampire novelty shop in town. It occurred to her then how funny it was that people had such a fascination with these wretched creatures; though she supposed the vampires that plagued the truck stop weren't exactly the type of fictional vampires that teenage girls went gaga over.

It so happened they had several dozen wooden stakes with the title of some upcoming vampire movie printed on them. She didn't care about the movie, but surprisingly the stakes seemed sturdy and had nice sharp points. They'd be perfect. Julie had smiled for the first time in days as she left the store with two large shopping bags filled to the brim with the novelty stakes.

Their shift started roughly an hour before the sun went down so the three busied themselves with hiding the stakes, while serving customers. Julie tried to decide if it being busy was a good or bad thing. For what they intended to do, they didn't want an audience, but at the same time she was terrified. The customers being there helped calm her rattled nerves.

She was certain that despite their recent differences, Veronica would assist them, or at the very least not interfere with their killing the others. Julie had already determined that Veronica could read minds, though she doubted the vamps knew about her ability, so Veronica would know Julie’s plan as soon as she stepped into the store.

Once done placing the stakes, Julie briskly walked over to the restaurant counter, where Sandy was ringing in a customer. *They* were coming and they were close, she could feel Tabitha's emotions. Julie took a quick head count of customers. There were still ten people in the restaurant and several people relaxing in the truckers’ lounge. That meant roughly thirteen humans, not including the trio of workers in the truck stop and the truckers sleeping in the trucks outside. The parking lot was nearly filled to capacity.

A trucker, a young-looking man in perhaps his mid-twenties, flirted with Sandy for a moment before strolling on out of the restaurant. Julie watched until he was out of earshot before leaning over to Sandy and whispering: "They are all placed, and *they're* almost here."

Sandy's face drained of all colour. She shook her head quickly back and forth. "I don't know if I can do this," she whispered back, beginning to panic.

Ricardo, hearing Julie by the counter came out of the kitchen to stand in a circle, behind the counter with Julie and Sandy. "We're ready?"

Julie gave him a tight smile. "Ready," she confirmed then added, "and they're almost here."

Sandy began to wring her fingers in front of her. "I...I don't think I can do this," tears filled her eyes as she looked back and forth from Ricardo to Julie.

"You'll be surprised what you can do when you're forced to," Julie assured her placing an encouraging hand on the younger woman's arm.

Ricardo slung an arm over her shoulders and hugged her close. She allowed herself to be comforted. "After tonight we get our lives back, Sand." He kissed the top of her head.

"Miss, we're ready to order," one of the truckers, who was having a late supper with three of his buddies called over to her. Julie scurried over to their table, clumsily flipping open her order pad as she walked. She openly admitted she was a shitty waitress. As she took their orders, she felt the vampires' emotions in her head intensify. Looking up and out of the glass window she saw them. They appeared out of the woods, walking with quick, powerful strides. Julie's hand began to tremble as it wrote the order down.

Calm yourself. Gotta remain calm. Clear headed. You can do this, she coached herself.

"Something wrong miss?" The oldest of the group nodded toward her hand when she lifted her eyes to meet his.

Julie did her best to give a light-hearted chuckle, which came out more like a squeak than anything. "I'm fine," she assured them, but she wasn't fooling anybody.

Who am I kidding? How the hell are we going to kill them? It's a fool's mission. But she knew they had to try. She was feeling Tabitha's emotions clearly now as the group crossed the interstate, looking as majestic and 'Vogue' magazine as they ever did. She could sense Tabitha had made a decision, and she was pretty certain she knew what that decision was. They all knew this day would come. The vampires were leaving, and leaving no witnesses in their wake.

"Is that all?" Julie asked looking from one trucker to the other, attempting to give them all a friendly smile, while trying to keep an eye on the vamps.

They shook their heads in reply.

"Good, coming right up boys," she turned on her heel and headed over to the kitchen window.

****

Jacob was pushing the truck to its limits as they sped towards the truck stop. If Devlon's premonition was correct, which he knew it would be, then they needed to get back there. And fast, before the group of vamps decided to jump ship. For his premonition to be true the vampires would need to leave soon in order to relocate themselves so they could prepare for the assassination. If they left before Jacob and Devlon could reach them, they might not see them again until the day *she*, Scarlet, killed their Queen.

"If you don't slow down, you'll end up wrecking the truck Jacob," Devlon advised. They blew past a sign that said 'Welcome to Maryland.' Jacob did the calculations in his head. One-hundred miles an hour, twenty miles, to the truck stop. Twelve minutes, give or take.

The sun had disappeared completely over the horizon, leaving faint traces of reds and oranges. The vampires would be up feeding by now if still in the area. *If.*

"We won't be able to get there any faster if we get stopped for speeding or crash," Devlon warned.

"We'll worry about that if it happens," Jacob shot back, not taking his eyes from the road. Looking down he noticed he was white knuckling the steering wheel. He loosened his grip slightly. "Go grab the weapons we're almost there."

"Fine," Devlon rose from his seat and made his way to the bunk of the cab. Moving the floor mat aside, he pushed a button which was cleverly hidden underneath. There was a faintly audible click. Hearing the click he settled the mat back down on the floor and went to the cab bed. He pulled the single-sized foam mattress from the frame and set it aside. Underneath it was a hidden compartment, now slightly raised - just enough that he could pull it up with the assistance of a knife or a hard, thin object. Pulling a knife from the small pantry overhead, he inserted it into the crack and pulled up on the lid, to reveal a compartment full of silver stakes. And a couple high tech fibreglass bows and arrows.

This wasn't the first time they'd had to deal with a group of the King’s vampires and he was certain it wouldn't be the last. "So, what are we taking?" He called over his shoulder. He felt the truck slowing down and pulling over to a rest stop which was a mile or so down the interstate from their destination.

"Take it all," Jacob called back, parking the truck and shutting down the engine.

****

They were killing the human truck stop workers tonight. Veronica had heard Tabitha's decision earlier that day. This was going to be their last night at the truck stop. Tabitha's plan was to feed, kill off Julie, Richardo and Sandy then burn the truck stop to the ground. There was to be no evidence, or trail. They'd go back and sleep the day away at the farm and then be on the road, headed as far away from New York City as possible the next night.

As they drew closer, and began to make their way across the I-95 Veronica started to pick up Julie and the others’ thoughts.

Julie: *Stakes are planted. We're ready for them.*

Sandy: *We're going to die, we're going to die. I hope to God that I can at least take Sebastian with me when I go.*

Ricardo: *Gotta protect the girls.*

Julie: *It's almost over. We can do this.*

They're going to get themselves killed, Veronica thought. *However, with my help maybe they can pull it off. Julie did almost kill Scarlet once*. She'd been racking her brain all day trying to figure a way out of this situation. Perhaps killing the vampires could be a possibility after all. The humans were currently living on borrowed time as it was, and they evidently knew it.

"We feed, and once everything is quiet; we find Julie, Richardo and Sandy and finish them off, then burn it all to the ground," Tabitha instructed as they reached the parking lot of the truck stop and made their way to the parked semi-trucks on the left side of the lot.

"Ha ha, it's goin' ta burn." Chyna's eyes danced with delight.

Sebastian laughed. "I want to finish Sandy off; been waiting a long time for that."

"That bitch Julie: I'm going to have so, *so* much fun with her," Scarlet snarled, involuntarily rubbing the area on her chest when she had been stabbed.

As they approached the trucks, Chyna eyed them all as she tapped her index finger against her metallic pink painted lips. Her lips perfectly matched the pink and silver sundress she was wearing. She wagged her finger at each of the trucks as she chanted, "eenie, meenie, miney, oh-oh-oh; you'll do." She giggled, and clapped her hands excitedly.

Chyna's finger landed on a silver and black transport marked 'Fast and Easy' on the trailer. The light was still on in the cab, signalling to them that the driver was still awake. Chyna was more of a seduce them kind of girl than an ambush them while they were sleeping sort.

Veronica remained silent. Now that she had an idea of what the humans inside had planned she needed to adjust her strategy accordingly. She then sensed there was an additional factor at work now, surprising and greatly welcomed. Somewhere hiding in the woods surrounding the truck stop, the vampires from last night were lurking.

She tried to tap into Jacob's thoughts. Almost there. *Almost.* His thoughts were so close they taunted her, like something you tried to remember, but couldn't quite get there. She growled to herself in frustration; he wasn't letting her in.

As much as their presence would pretty much ensure the humans' survival, her own she wasn't so sure about. Despite not being able to get into his thoughts she could pretty much guess what their plan was, and the outcome didn't look too promising for her.

****

"They're planning on killing the vampires," Jacob chuckled softly as he whispered the information to his younger brother who was presently crouching next to him in the woods. The brothers had a perfect view of the vampires as they made their way into the truck parking. They watched as the vampires all disappeared into separate trucks for their nightly feeding.

Devlon snickered beside him. "It's a damned good thing we showed up then. They would have gotten their little mortal asses killed."

Jacob was silent for a moment, listening to the vampires' thoughts. "We're just in time. The vampires are planning on feeding, killing the humans then torching the place. We would have lost the chance to kill them." He placed a hand on his brother's shoulder, "Good job brother, I can assure you the Queen will be very pleased when we meet up with her."

Devlon nodded. "What's the plan?"

Jacob patted the bow he had in his hand. "Once they finish feeding we take them out as they leave the trucks. Quick, easy and we're out of here. Primary target is Scarlet. Next Sebastian, Tabitha, Chyna and finally... Veronica.'

"What? Wait. Veronica?" Devlon looked at his brother slightly confused, "Why? She could be useful. Didn't you say earlier she was different to the others?"

"Devlon," Jacob sighed as he shook his head slowly, "she's of *his* bloodline, part of a group planning on killing the Queen. We're taking no chances. She dies." His tone indicated that the discussion was closed for debate.

...we take them out as they leave the trucks. Quick, easy and we're out of here. Primary target is Scarlet. Next Sebastian, Tabitha, Chyna and finally... Veronica. The thoughts echoed in Veronica's head as she drank from the neck of the lucky trucker

who owned a Light blue Volvo with the logo, 'We get it there fast' written across the trailer.

Shit! She cursed angrily to herself as she lifted her head, licking the blood from her lips. She still had no idea where in the woods they were. The attack could come from anywhere. *They're going to take us out as we leave the trucks. Fine, then I just won't leave the truck,* she decided. She smiled to herself, it was as good a plan as any; simple, but brilliant in its simplicity.

"There is movement by the black International," Devlon whispered to Jacob, preparing his bow to fire.

"Which one is it," Jacob whispered back.

Devlon crept a little closer. "One of the females," he crept closer still, then grinned, "Bingo! It's Scarlet."

"Take her out," Jacob commanded at his side.

Devlon aimed, pulling the arrow as taut as possible, ensuring maximum speed and power, and then released.

They watched as the arrow sailed through the air, barrelling towards the unsuspecting vampire. Just before the arrow made contact, Scarlet seemed to *see* them. But it made no difference. The arrow made contact with amazing force, hitting her in the chest. Perfect shot, upper left hand side. She screamed, clutching at the arrow as she fell to the ground.

"Killer shot. One down," Devlon announced.

"Four more to go," Jacob patted his brother on the shoulder and then prepared himself for the vampires to come charging out of the other trucks.

****

"Something is going on out there, come see," Julie motioned for Ricardo and Sandy to come over and join her at the window to peer out in the direction of the trucks. She'd been watching the trucks like a hawk since the vampires disappeared into them. The several customers still lounging around the restaurant and truckers' lounge were of no interest to her now. All that mattered were the vamps.

Richardo and Sandy both hurried over to her, one taking up position at each of her sides. "Where?" asked Richardo.

She pointed to the black International. "There. I think it was Scarlet. She came out of the truck, stood for a moment, then Wham-O!" Julie slapped her palms together making a clapping sound. "She sort of shrieked, seemed to grab at her chest, then toppled down to the ground."

"Do you think she's dead?" Sandy asked, with a faint glimmer of hope in her voice.

Julie shrugged, "We can only hope."

Moments later they watched Sebastian, Tabitha and Chyna rush from the trucks. Sebastian came sprinting towards the restaurant, towards them, just as something appeared to go sailing past him, missing him by inches.

Chyna was the next to fall victim to whatever was happening outside. Her fate ended in much the same way as Scarlet: an arrow through the heart. She screamed, clawed at her chest then collapsed to the ground.

The arrow meant for Tabitha missed completely. Julie and the others watched as she made a run for the woods, actually running towards the arrows!

"What the hell is she doing?" Ricardo asked, perplexed by her actions.

"Dealing with the assassins as I come for the hostages," a deep, vicious voice snarled from behind them.

"Sebastian," Sandy gasped as he grabbed her roughly and threw her over his left shoulder.

"If they want to put an arrow through my heart they'll have to go through you," he snarled, slapping her not so tenderly on the ass.

Sandy cried out, beating her fists on his back as he carried her over his shoulder, across the restaurant.

"Hey, wait just a minute there buddy," One of the remaining truckers in the restaurant, stood and started to make his way over to Sebastian and Sandy.

"If you value your life you'll sit your redneck ass back down," Sebastian snarled, eyes blazing red and fangs bared.

The man froze in mid-stride, his eyes shining with terror, as he began to back away from Sebastian and Sandy his hands out to the sides in surrender, head bowed.

****

Tabitha slammed into Devlon with the force of a freight train, sending him spiralling backwards into a nearby tree, his bow went sailing out of reach. He fell against the tree then to the forest floor with a thump, but was on his feet in seconds, pulling a stake from under his belt.

They both circled each other, sizing each other up. Devlon looked up and noticed his brother coming to his aid. "Don't worry I have this, finish the rest of them off," he yelled out to Jacob.

Jacob hesitated for a moment, realized that Devlon had taken on much stronger than the likes of Tabitha before and headed off in search of the vampire that shared his special gift. She was the only one that hadn't exited the trucks upon hearing Scarlet scream. *Cleaver little minx got into my head after all,* he thought with a slight grin creeping onto his face.

Once in the parking lot he stood silently, listening for her thoughts and coming up empty. "I'm going to find you Veronica, might as well come out and get it over with," Jacob finally announced. In truth, he was rather enjoying this little cat and mouse game she was playing with him. He'd find her, no doubt at all in his mind. Then he'd kill her.

****

Sebastian tossed Sandy into the ceramic tiled floor and jumped on top over her, pinning her hands over her head, with one of his own large hands. His eyes flashed with hunger and anger as they took her in, lingering on her breasts, then her neck.

"Who is out there in the woods my precious?" Sebastian demanded, his lips less than an inch from her ear.

Sandy shook her head. "I don't know," she said. Her eyes filled with tears. "I don't know."

"Perhaps this will jog your memory," he suggested as his fangs sank into the tender, creamy flesh.

She started to cry out, but his free hand covered her mouth, preventing her from making a sound. Her body writhed and bucked against his, but to no avail. He was too big, too powerful.

"Stay here and keep watch", Julie whispered to Ricardo as she snatched up the stake which she had secured under the cash counter and headed toward the kitchen, as quietly as she could. Aware of a vampire's keen senses she doubted she would have the element of surprise on her side, but she had to try.

As she entered the kitchen she was horrified to see Sebastian on top of the squirming Sandy, draining her. If he had heard her enter the room then he didn't let on. Creeping up slowly behind him, it seemed to take an eternity to finally position herself over him. She raised the stake high above her head and sent it barrelling down toward him, hoping to pierce his heart through his back.

Chapter 10

Just as the stake was about to make contact with his flesh he jerked upward, turning to her, his eyes fierce, mouth covered in Sandy's blood. It dripped down the side of his jowl and onto his chin. His hand shot up and grasped Julie's wrist, bending her arm back.

Julie screamed out in shock and pain, as she dropped the stake to the floor. She heard a snap and felt the hot, searing pain run up the length of her arm as it broke. His other arm, which had been pinning Sandy's arms to the floor, shot out and grabbed Julie by the neck.

He slowly stood up, still holding Julie by the neck with a single arm, leaving Sandy choking on the floor. "You fucking whore. I've been wanting to do this since I first laid eyes on you," he growled as he began to choke the life from her.

Her legs dangled several inches from the floor. She clawed at his hand, holding tight to her neck, crushing her windpipe, with her one still good hand. She gasped for air that never seemed to come. She could feel the bones in her neck preparing to crumble under his strong grip. She closed her eyes and, as she started to black out, she felt him release her. She fell hard to the floor, her forehead bouncing off the edge of one of the stainless steel tables in the center of the room. She felt the warmth of the blood trickle down her temple.

Julie felt something hard and heavy fall beside her. Opening her eyes she saw Sebastian's red eyes, cold and vacant staring into hers. Julie gasped and tried to wriggle away from him, but was stopped by the table on which she had bashed her forehead. Looking up she was shocked to see Sandy kneeling over Sebastian's body, a blank expression on her face, holding one of the stakes Julie had given her. The stake was dripping with blood, Sebastian's blood.

Good girl, Julie thought as blackness overtook her.

****

"You'll never stop him now," Tabitha sneered.

"I'll worry about the King another day. It's your head I want tonight," Devlon taunted back.

Both were weak and badly beaten. Both had got in their fair share of blows on the other over the past ten minutes or so. The forest floor was covered in their blood as they circled each other yet again.

"Not today," Tabitha announced taking a lunge for Devlon. Her teeth sank into his neck as she propelled him backwards onto the bloody forest floor. He moaned as hot searing pain, shot down his neck. He was losing strength by the second. One hand caught her long dark curly locks and he attempted to pull her head off him by yanking at her hair. His other hand searched the forest floor some something, anything with which to kill her.

He grew weaker and weaker, getting to the point where he was quite certain he might pass out. Then he had it, something long, hard and metallic. It was one of his arrows. Grasping it with his free hand he whipped his arm around and forced it through the left side of her back and into her heart.

Tabitha lifted her head from his neck and cried out. He could feel his blood, dripping from her mouth and onto his neck and face. He gave her dead body a shove to get her off him. He attempted to sit up, found himself to be too weak and collapsed back to the cold forest floor.

Jacob, I need you, he thought hoping his brother would hear his plea.

****

While Jacob was searching the trucks, Veronica had managed to sneak out of the one she was in and make her way into the woods. She knew now that all the vampires she had once reluctantly called her family were dead. She was the last one standing, and she planned to keep it that way. The humans were safe and she was now finally free of the monsters that had, on a certain level, kept her captive these past few months.

She was just far enough away from the truck stop that she was beginning to feel safe when she heard him. *Jacob, I need you*, the vampire's thoughts were pleading, desperate. "They were going to kill you Veronica, don't be stupid," she told herself out loud. She took a few more steps away from the truck stop...away from the pleading, presumably dying vampire. Then she stopped.

Her conscience got the better of her.

"Damn it!" she growled. Turning she ran in the direction from which she felt the thoughts were coming. And there she found him; the younger brother. He was lying spread-eagled on the ground, blood covering his body, with a pile of ash, which she assumed was once Tabitha, beside him.

Devlon looked up at her. "I need blood," he choked out, as his eyes closed shut. He was near death. Part of her was furious with him and his brother. They wouldn't have thought twice about killing her off. She was part of the plan, they just hadn't caught her. But the other part - the part of her that still longed to be human - commanded her to save him.

Heaving a loud, expressive sigh, Veronica walked over to him and fell to her knees beside him. Biting into her wrist she lowered the open wound to his mouth. "Drink," she commanded.

He clutched onto her arm and drank deeply. After several minutes he seemed satisfied, releasing her arm. His body began to rejuvenate before her eyes. "Thank you," he whispered, opening his eyes to look up at her.

Before she could answer him a voice boomed behind her. "Step away from him," it commanded.

Startled, Veronica leapt to her feet, spinning around to face the direction of the voice. It was Jacob. He stood roughly twenty feet away from them, his bow aimed at her heart.

"I guarantee if you try to run, my arrow will be faster," he threatened when he noticed her contemplating making a run for it.

Devlon pushed himself to his feet, putting himself in front of Veronica. "Put the arrow down, brother."

"Move out of the way, Devlon," Jacob ordered.

"No. I won't allow you to kill her," Devlon, looked at his brother defiantly. "She saved my life. I owe her hers."

Jacob hesitated before lowering his weapon. "Fine. Have it your way. The rest are dead. We need to go. Now. We don't have time to argue about it." He began to walk through the woods towards the rest station they had left their truck, and then stopped short and turned back to face Devlon and Veronica. "Her actions will be on you," he warned giving Devlon a stern look. Having said his part, Jacob continued walking back to the truck.

"Come on. Let's go," Devlon gave her a soft smile and motioned for her to follow them.

Veronica hesitated. She still had a lot to learn about what she was. *Who* she now was. She wasn't going to get that information on her own; she had a feeling they could help her find the answers she'd been searching for.

"Where are we going?" Veronica asked, jogging up behind them to catch up.

"New York City," Devlon replied.

New York City, she thought smiling inwardly. He had just said the magic words.

****

Julie regained consciousness to find herself in an ambulance and on the move. Ricardo and Sandy were sitting on a bench beside her stretcher. They were both bandaged, and looked like death twice over, but alive - that was the main thing. She attempted to struggle to sit up, but Sandy placed a hand on her chest to urge her back down.

"We're taking you to the hospital. The paramedics think you'll be alright, but they want to run some tests, just to be safe," Sandy explained.

"And they need to fix your arm," Ricardo added.

Julie sighed and nodded. There was silence for the next several minutes as Julie tried to gather her thoughts. The events of the night seemed jumbled in her head. Foggy.

Vampires! Panicked, Julie attempted to sit up again. Sandy once again placed a hand on her chest, urging her back down. "Are they gone? Are they dead?" Julie demanded.

Sandy gave her a smile. "I think so. We're safe."

"They must be. We no longer feel the urge to be at the truck stop." Richardo added. He leaned over and brushed a lock of hair from Julie's face, tucking it behind her ear. "We're free."

Julie could feel tears well up in her eyes and trickle down her temples. *Free! We're finally free!* The horrors of the past few months seemed to fade away. They were free at last.

****

Ned Young slowed his small white International semi-truck down as he approached a woman walking alone along the highway. Once he reached her, he stopped the truck fully, leaned over to the passenger side and pushed open the door. He peered out at the woman before him.

She was an attractive woman. He guessed in her mid-thirties. Dark hair, slim, average height, with some sexy curves. He usually didn't pick up hitchhikers, but he was lonely and he hadn't been laid in a long, long time. Perhaps if he was nice to her and offered her a lift she'd offer him a little something in return.

"Where are you heading sweetheart?" Ned asked, giving her his winning smile.

The woman hesitated as if considering the question. Finally, she answered, "New York City."

"Then hop on in Sweetheart, I'll give you a lift." He pushed the door open further and sat back upright in his seat.

"I’d appreciate that." She smiled up at him, then hoisted herself up into the seat beside him.

"It's dangerous out there, fer a pretty lady like you. Lotta dangerous people around."

The woman nodded. "I can take care of myself."

"So... What's your name honey? I'm Ned," he introduced himself extending his large, meaty hand to her.

She smiled at him seductively, licking her ruby red lips before answering. "Good to meet you Ned," she took his large hand, "You can call me... Scarlet."

The End

The Everett Vampires Fact Sheet

* The exact age and origin of vampires is unknown, the two oldest vampires are considered the mother and father of all vampires. The King Griffith and the Queen Louisa. There is speculation that the King and Queen were created by God as vampires originally and had never lived a human life.

* The King and Queen have not been mates for over 2000 years. Their differences in ideologies has caused a rift between both them and their aligning clans.

* The vampires sired from the Kings bloodline are considered the "Kings Clan." Vampires from the Kings Clan are considered to bc more ruthless, aggressive and rely more on instinct and feral urges then on reason and intellect. If a vampire from the Kings bloodline is provoked their eyes will turn red. When a vampire from the Kings bloodline turns a human there is a great chance the newborn will become more beast then human.

* The vampires sired from the Queens bloodline are considered to be of the "Queens Clan." Vampires born of the Queens bloodline are generally stronger, more skilled and mentally stable then those of the Kings Clan. It is speculated that the reason vampires of the Queens Clan are more in control of their feral side and are born more advanced physically, mentally and emotionally

is due to the selective turning of humans by the Queen over the centuries. When a vampire of the Queens bloodline is provoked their eyes will turn white.

* When a human is turned in most cases they will obtain a special ability upon being turned. Normally the special ability will be in direct relation to their skills and abilities as a human. For instance, a human that is naturally intuitive may become clairvoyant as a vampire.

* As a vampire ages throughout the decades and centuries they will develop a resistance to the sunlight. For instance, the King and Queen are virtually immune to the sunlight's rays. However, like with human genetics a newborn vampire may develop a sunlight resistance quite quickly if they are turned by an ancient or by the King or Queen. The older the siring vampire is the stronger and more developed the newborn will be.

* While there is currently no war between the two vampire clans there is animosity between the two sides, the racial divide between the clans has been widening as the centuries pass.

* Only three things can kill a vampire. Decapitation, Stake through the heart or being drained of blood. Many younger vampires can also be killed when exposed to sunlight.

For more information on Everett Vampires or other Everett Supernaturals visit: www.elixaeverett.com

Soft & Hard Erotic Publishing

www.elixaeverett.com

Contact Information

Website: www.elixaeverett.com

Email: terry towers@hotmail.ca

Facebook: Terry Towers

Twitter: TerryTowersXXX

Works By Terry Towers

Available Now - Singles

Frat Party Partner Swap

Under the Officer's Command

Daddy's Special Christmas Gift

All For Daddy (Taboo Edition)

The Marine's Naughty Sister (Taboo Edition)

Little Virgin Sister's Webcam Show (Taboo Edition)

Doing Her For Dad (Taboo Edition)

Deceiving Him (The Billionaires' BDSM Sex Club)

Her Brother, Her Hero

Her 'What if' Guy (Pursued By The Billionaire)

The Inheritance: Anything He Craves

Available Now - Themed Singles

Taken By The Team (Humiliation And Gangbang Fantasies Fulfilled)

Taken By The Marines (Humiliation, Gangbang And Cuckold Fantasies Fulfilled)

The Cop And The Girl From The Coffee Shop

The Politician And The Girl From The Coffee Shop

The Assassin And The Girl From The Coffee Shop

The Bounty Hunter And The Girl From The Coffee Shop

The Firefighter And The Girl From The Coffee Shop

The CEO And The Girl From The Coffee Shop

The Porn Star And The Girl From The Coffee Shop

Available Now - Series

Hitching A Ride

Hitching A Ride 2: To Trust A Con

Conjugal Visits

Conjugal Visits 2: New Beginnings

Sibling Rivalry

Sibling Rivalry 2: Never Say Never

Sibling Rivalry 3: In It Together

Moan For Uncle

Moan For Uncle 2: Keeping It Secret

Moan For Uncle 3: No More Secrets

Moan For Uncle 4: Skeletons In The Closet

Moan For Uncle 5: Love Or Duty

Moan For Uncle 6: To Love And Honour

Available Now - Mirror Editions

(Please note Mirror Editions are mainstream non-PI editions of some of Terry's bestselling taboo works.)

Doing Her For The Boss (Rewrite of Doing Her For Dad)

The Marine's Naughty Sister (Rewrite of The Marine's Naughty Neighbour)

The Virgin's Webcam Show (rewrite of Little Virgin Sister's Webcam Show)

Seducing Blake (Rewrite of All For Daddy)

Now Available - Bundles

The Terry Towers' Taboo Collection Vol. 1

The Terry Towers' Taboo Collection Vol. 2

Naughty But Nice Mirror Edition Collection

The Moan For Uncle Bundle (Books 1-3)

The Sibling Rivalry Bundle (Books 1-3)

German Language Versions

Taken By The Team (Humiliation and Gangbang Fantasies Fulfilled)

Von der Mannschaft Durchgenommen (Erniedrigungs- und Gangbangfantasien erfüllt)

Taken By The Marines (Humiliation, Gangbang & Cuckold Fantasies Fulfilled)

Von den Marines durchgenommen (Erniedrigungs- und Gangbang- & Fremdgehfantasien erfüllt)

The Marine's Naughty Sister

Die unanständige Schwester des Marines

Moan For Uncle

Sehnsucht nach dem Onkel

Hitching A Ride: Sexy Anhalter (Anrüchiges einverständnis erotik)

Sibling Rivalry

Geschwister Rivalität

All For Daddy

Alles für Papa

Italian Language Versions

Taken By The Team (Humiliation and Gangbang Fantasies Fulfilled)

Abusata dal gruppo (Umiliazione e Fantasie di Gangbang Soddisfatte)

Moan For Uncle

Un gemito per lo zio

Her Brother, Her Hero

Suo fratello, il suo eroe

Spanish Language Versions

Taken By The Team (Humiliation and Gangbang Fantasies Fulfilled)

Abusada por el equipo (Humillación y fantasías de sexo realizadas en grupo)

Moan For Uncle

El deseo prohibido

French Language Versions

Taken By The Team (Humiliation and Gangbang Fantasies Fulfilled)

Prise Par L'équipe (Fantasmes Assouvis D'humiliation Et De Viol Collectif)

Coming Soon

Moan For Hubby (Moan For Uncle 7)

The Politician And The Girl From The Coffee Shop 2: All That Glitters

Works By Nikki Nexus

Available Now - Singles

Daddy Says: Ménage Sex Games

Santa's Brothel

The Confessional: The Naughty Nuns Series

The Fire Eater

Taken By The Team (Humiliation And Gangbang Fantasies Fulfilled)

Taken By The Marines (Humiliation, Gangbang And Cuckold Fantasies Fulfilled)

Available Now - Bundles

Naughty But Nice Mirror Edition Collection

Coming Soon

Taken By The Mob (Humiliation And Gangbang Fantasies Fulfilled)

German Language Versions

Daddy Says: Ménage Sex Games

Papa sagt:Jetzt ein flotter Dreier

Works By Adrian Athens

Available Now

The Welding Instructor

Melting Point

Coming Soon

Men For Sale

Works By Elixa Everett

Available Now - Singles

Escort With 1000 Faces

Lust, Love & Luck

I Conjure Thee (Enslaved To The Djinn)

Midnight Encounter - Seduced By A Vampire (Quickie)

Tag, The Vampire's Game

Erotic Flash: A Vampire's Seduction

Children Of The Vampire King (Non-erotic horror)

Available Now - Series

A Night At Club Vampire

A Night At Club Vampire 2: Nigel

Visions Of The Vampire Queen (Book 1 Of The Vampire Queen Series)

Available Now - Bundles

Vampire Whispers - (Bundle of 4 Erotic Vampire Stories)

Coming Soon

Return Of The Vampire Queen (Book 2 Of The Vampire Queen Series)

German Language Versions

Midnight Encounter - Seduced By A Vampire

Mitternächtliche Begegnung: Von einem Vampir verführt

Works By Angelique Ambers

Available Now - Singles

Forced Into Submission (Her Fantasy, His Pleasure)

German Language Versions

Forced Into Submission (Her Fantasy, His Pleasure)

Mit Gewalt unterworfen (Ihre Träume, sein Vergnügen)

Printed in Great Britain
by Amazon

58613337R00096